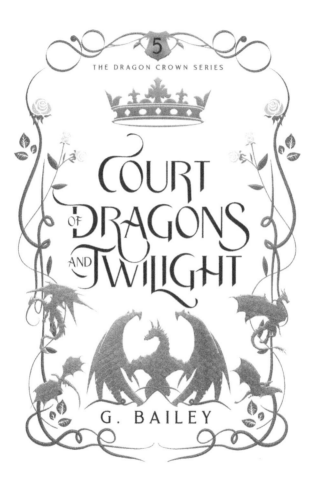

5

THE DRAGON CROWN SERIES

COURT OF DRAGONS AND TWILIGHT

G. BAILEY

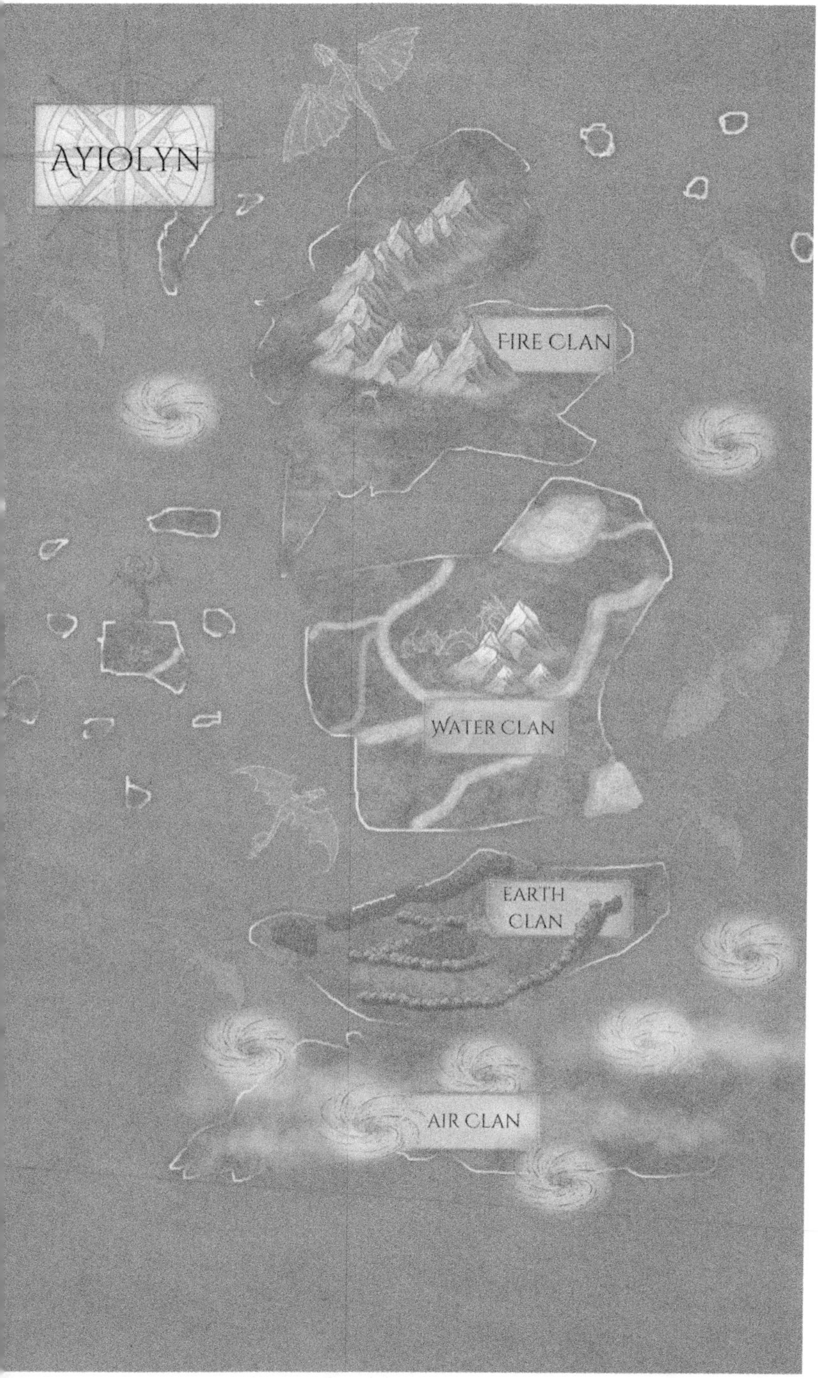
AYIOLYN
FIRE CLAN
WATER CLAN
EARTH CLAN
AIR CLAN

COURT OF DRAGONS AND TWILIGHT

THE DRAGON CROWN SERIES
BOOK FIVE

G. BAILEY

CONTENTS

 Created with Vellum

DESCRIPTION

One queen for Ayiolyn.
Will the power of five dragons be able to stop
the gods?

After the surprise attack, Emrys is lost, and it's
not only him trapped in the Air Court. I am
offered one more trial, and the winner takes the
world. This time, I won't be the only one facing
Aphrodite's trials.

Each king has been given a trial to conquer,
with the goddess of love utilizing their fears.
The clock is ticking and every day that passes,
Emrys soul grows weaker.
Arden, Emrys, Grayson, Lysander, and Terrin

are my world. After everything we have gotten through, we cannot lose now.

I was born to be a spirit queen and thrive in the shadows. To win, I will need every element and my mates, or everything will be lost.

This is a full-length enemy-to-lovers fantasy romance with dragon shifters, a badass heroine, and possessive alpha males. Perfect for fans of spicy fantasy whychoose? romance. This is book five and the final book of the Dragon Crown series; the books must be read in order.

PROLOGUE

HERA

*M*any would stumble through surprise portals that open right below them, but the wolf queen, she steps through with enough grace to make every soul stand to attention. The wolf queen, who has ruled this world for many years, holds her head high as she faces us. I'm used to humans and mortals, who show little respect to gods these days, but she still comes across as respectful even as she faces us down. She's dressed casually in soft brown clothes, and yet there's an eerie sense of dark magic tied to her soul. It comes from her mates, from the dark god they are bound to and his pit of hell. This wolf is tied to Persephone, and I know enough of that goddess to know she would not have bound herself to a wolf shifter she didn't know was good.

She brushes her long blonde hair over her shoulder and looks at both Cronus and me. Cronus tightens his fingers, woven between mine, and I let myself glance his way for just a second. Cronus was my first love, and to this day, I can see him how he looked when was young, and yet I think he is handsome either way. I remember the day I met Cronus for the first time, how his dark gaze swelled my heart and made it burst open with joy. How I knew deep down we were meant for each other, bound by the fate of love and all the stars that lined up to bring us together for just that moment. It wasn't to be. We couldn't be anything to each other back then. The world was at war, and I was hidden away in another world. I loved my time on Earth, and I loved my human husband very much. He was the father of my child, and I will forever cherish the time we had together, but sometimes, I found myself dreaming of Cronus. Wondering if he dreamt of me.

He told me he did. That he never stopped searching the world for me. Cronus is the one that I truly fell in love with first. Our fates were divided, torn apart, and yet here we are; we found each other again in an old world, and we will not be parted until Hades accepts us both into the afterlife.

Even locked in here, thousands of miles from her mates, a frightening howl echoes through the air. Queen Mairin smiles. "They will rip you apart when they get here, and it will not be long. I would quickly decide why you opened a portal in my granddaughter's bedroom and summoned me here. I was watching her."

Cronus smiles at the queen, who is young and nothing more than a child in our years. Cronus told me he watched her from the shadows as she saved this world and made sure that peace is all the world will know for generations. Out of respect for her, he called her here, even though he hates most people other than me. "I believe introductions may be in order," Cronus begins. "You may have been linked to Persephone's soul, and I can still sense her power throughout you, but do not test my patience by using that power here. As for your mates, they can be greeted by my guards."

"Cronus," I gently warn.

"I would not call that power in my presence. I admire you, Queen, for the fight you had on your hands in your early years, but I am Cronus, and this is Hera. We are gods and we will not be tested," he continues in a more pleasant tone.

I tug my eyes to hers. "Cronus means to say you are not in any danger, and we want to speak to you about an important matter. Tell your mates you will be returned shortly."

Her eyes flash green for a moment, and she crosses her arms. "They will come for me no matter what I say, but if they are harmed…I do not care what kind of god you are, you will die." She threatens the father of gods, one of the most powerful beings in the world, without an inch of fear on her face. "I'm well aware what gods reside in my world, Cronus and Hera. I'm unaware of why you've called me here."

"I see why you like this one. She's sharp and to the point." I lean my head on Cronus's shoulder, noting his mint scent. I slip into Mai's mind, as she likes to call herself, to see if she can be trusted and find my answer quickly. She is loyal and trustworthy, and she hates lies. I can read all of her mind, just slightly, and yet it's still like a brick wall is wrapped tight around her

4

innermost thoughts and those concerning her mates. She's had a past full of pain, but she knows love. Love is exactly how we are going to get her to help us.

"My daughter and granddaughter are in trouble, and while I reside in your world, I cannot help them," I begin with brutal honesty, because from glimpsing into her mind, I know she can sense lies like a superpower. "Cronus took me from my granddaughter, but now we are mated. We are family and he wants to secure her world alongside me."

Mai turns her knowing gaze to Cronus. "Is this true?" She needs to hear it from him, and I don't blame her.

He looks right at me, and my heart leaps. "I am devoted to Hera."

I lean in and kiss him softly before turning to Mai. "Mai, I need the staff to return to Ayiolyn and to my family. There are two gods who are both extremely dangerous, and if we don't stop them in Ayiolyn, then they will come to other worlds. They will bleed into the universe and spread nothing but horror and war. Your world is at peace. Let us go back and secure another world of peace."

"Was Princess Ellelin not able to do this herself?"

I think of the flash Cronus showed me of the spirit castle, under attack by dragons and men. "No, she needs help. She shouldn't stand alone. Let us show her how to fight with gods against gods, rather than gods winning an unfair battle. I will not see her die. We're going to go through with Cronus's dead army, secure the lands, and live there peacefully."

Mai tenses at the mention of the army. She didn't know about it. "You want me to send you, two powerful gods, through with an army, to another world, with the assurance that you're not going to take over because you have family there?"

"Child," Cronus growls. "Are you aware of who you stand before? I've sat in your world for a very long time, and I have not interfered when I could simply send my army out of these doors and take over. I watched you rise from the girl who couldn't shift and was in love with four men bound to Hades, even when she knew they couldn't be hers. I watched your life with your memories gone, I watched who hunted you and who loved you. I witnessed your darkest and greatest moments, and they are still nothing but a blink of time to me. If you wish to call me a liar, you will find only you hold that title, Mai."

Her eyes widen and she goes still as she realises just how powerful my mate is. A smart queen would want us out of their world as quickly as possible. Loud, dark growls echo from outside the doors. Her mates are impressive to get here so quickly. Cronus sighs. "Your wolves are going to damage my castle."

Mai arches an eyebrow. "Let them in, then."

Cronus laughs. "If you want them dead, then—"

"No," I interrupt Cronus before he can say another word.

A silence echoes between us, only the sound of wolves hounding at the door to fill the silence. Queen Mai is smart, and she doesn't shock me. "If I say no, you'll come and get the staff either way, I assume."

"That is correct. We're showing you respect, considering you were respectful to our kin," I explain. "And Cronus told me you are nothing short of a hero to this world. I do not want to leave here on bad terms and break the agreement my granddaughter put in place. She gave

7

you the staff, and that deal is worth a discussion before action."

The doors break down and four massive wolves run in, straight to their queen's side. She holds her hand up. "I'm okay and I just made a deal with these gods. They are leaving our world."

The biggest black wolf presses against her side before all of them wait for her next move. I'm impressed they have gotten past all the magic barriers Cronus lazily leaves lying about. I have a suspicion he really didn't try hard to keep them out. She holds out her hand. The staff appears, shimmering within a bright red magic. "One of my mates hid it really well in this bracelet. There are many magical devices he makes, but this locked it away." I sense its horrid power now. "I will send you through, but the staff stays in this world. That's not changing. We are closer to destroying it once and for all, and then there will be no way back. Do you understand?"

"We are not returning," Cronus answers for us both. We have discussed our plan in length after Cronus explained he can break the magic protection on Ayiolyn to stop me from entering.

"We are ready when you are, queen of the wolves."

Mai holds the staff up in the air, and magic blasts out the top like a star bursting in the night sky. A huge glowing portal spreads across the far wall, and beyond it shimmers another world. It's not Ayiolyn at all; it's one I don't know. It's not Earth either. All I can see is a shimmering expanse of blue sea with dozens of islands dotted around. Each of the islands looks like they're a different season. But winter seems huge, and right in the centre, the icy white trees spreading out like a wave to the other islands. She taps it again with green glowing eyes, and it shimmers, changing to the Spirit Court castle from outside on a field marked with dead dragons, ash and more death. We may be too late. Cronus hears and feels my heart racing, and we both rise to our feet as he links his arm around my waist.

The doors slam open next to the portal, and an army of literally dead skeletons start clicketing their way through the main hall to the portal. Queen Mai's eyes are widened slightly, but she doesn't show any reaction to using the staff or the army. She is very powerful to hold that staff so easily, but as I look closer, I see her wolves glowing the same colour, and they are all tense. They are sharing their power with her to control it.

I walk over to her and bow my head. Her eyes glow and she smiles once. "We won't be back to this world, and no one ever will. Have an everlasting, peaceful future, Queen Mairin of the Wolves."

I don't look back as I join Cronus and walk with his army into the world of dragons.

CHAPTER 1

Fire burns across the cloudy night sky like a comet, and I can do nothing but watch as it burns. It burns and spits flames, the fire endless and so bright it hurts to look at even for a moment, but I lie on the battlefield, and I do not move. I don't dare pull my eyes away as I watch dragons fall from the skies, as I see my people die before they really even got to live. I see my mate standing in the ash and smoke, but his eyes are not the same anymore. Emrys is gone… Did I follow his soul to death?

"You're not dying while I still breathe, my mate."

Lysander's command is sharp, demanding as

he always is, but each drop of his voice is filled with worry, and it pulls me from my daydream, or day nightmare. I force my tired eyes open for him, seeing my water king mate covered in blood and ash, burns and soot from head to toe. He is concentrating, and it takes me a moment to realise he is focused on me. Healing me. I nearly cough on the thick smoke in the air of our bedroom, even with the windows closed and the castle humming a song of death through the air. Lysander speaks out loud to whoever else is in the room. "She's awake, Arden." He might have been speaking out loud the first time to me. I don't know. Everything feels so strange to me.

"Thank fuck." Arden's weight dips the bed on my other side, and he cups my cheek with his hand that's black with ash. "Princess, you... What happened out there?"

"We should never have left her alone," Lysander snarls at Arden.

Arden is calm on the outside, but he feels like a fiery tornado through the bond. "She wasn't alone, and she was ambushed. We never could have known the tsar had powers or sided with Aphrodite." Arden looks at me once more, and his fiery red eyes are filled with the fire I feel from him. "I'm sorry, Elle. Fuck, we...I messed up. Are you alright? When you're ready, we need you to tell me where Emrys is, because he isn't here. I got a hint of his scent near where we found you, but he wasn't there."

My heart feels like it's racing harder and harder the more I think about Emrys... How do I tell them? What do I even say?

"Give her a second," Lysander growls before helping me sit up on the bed with Arden's help too. Every bit of movement hurts, and I didn't realise how injured I was from the fall until I moved. My throat is burning and sore, even with Lysander's healing, as I clear it a few times. Lysander touches my neck, pure water flowing around his hand and my throat. "We found you alone and nearly dead, Elle. I nearly fucking lost you, and I want to know exactly who tried to stop you from breathing."

"Emrys," I croak. Lysander drops his hand in shock, and Arden's eyes actually glow red. Like flames. "He...he isn't Emrys anymore."

Arden throws his head back. "What exactly happened? Emrys would rather die than hurt you...but he did this?"

I nod, remembering the feeling of not being

15

able to breathe, of how all the air in the world had just vanished for me. I really thought I was going to die, and I don't know why Ares didn't kill me. A dragon roar outside has me shooting my eyes to the window. Arden strokes my hand. "Everything's secure, Elle. The ward is back up, and that's your people out there. We've killed anybody else that was inside, but the rest of the army is outside the ward. Terrin tells me we have a lot of injuries, but we have portals open to the Water Court, and healers are rushing in, guided by Kian."

"Grayson?" I need to see him. After Emrys...I need my mates. I feel Terrin in the skies just outside the castle, but his thoughts are quiet to me. He hasn't blocked me out well enough, because I feel the waves of pure guilt coming off him. He is blaming himself for all of this.

"Gray is helping out in the field, and you can reach for him—"

Arden pauses when I shake my head. "I can't. Since I've woken up, the bond is silent. Can you reach me?"

They both focus on me, but when I hear nothing, I'm certain it's the same. I can sort of feel them, what they are feeling, but not connect to them anymore. Something is messing with our bond, and I'd bet money on it that Ares has done it.

"Fuck, how is that possible?" Lysander snaps at Arden.

"How the fuck would I know?" Arden is tense.

I burst into tears, and it stops them both. I put my hand up to stop them both from reaching for me. If I let them hold me, I won't get the words out. "Ares fully took over Emrys with Aphrodite's help. She knew and planned all of Ares's death. She wanted an elemental king's body, and I don't know if there's anything left of Emrys at all now." I can barely get the truth out through my tears. "There's nothing when I feel for him. I don't feel the bond or anything from him. Nothing!" I start rambling over my words. "I've lost him. I've—" Arden pulls me to him even when I fight, and Lysander wraps his arms around my back, holding me tight as I scream and cry, as the bitter taste of regret and horror of losing Emrys floods my mouth.

I don't know how long passes before I stop crying enough to hear what Arden is saying.

"He's not gone. Look at me, princess." He cups my cheek and turns my head up. "Emrys is not gone, just taken over, and we will fix him. There is no world where we give up on the air king. Don't give up on us, princess. Not now, not ever. We are your dragon kings, your elements, and we fly with you."

Closing my eyes, I rest my forehead on Arden's shoulder. "He was scared. I felt the moment that Ares took over him, and Emrys was scared. I couldn't help him."

Lysander brushes my hair over my shoulder, the black and purple waves flowing down my back. "He was scared for you. Not himself. Emrys always put you first from the moment he fell in love with you. He will fight Ares with everything he has, and so will we. None of us are going to give up until his body is actually dead, and he's not dead yet."

Grayson comes in, his shoulders dropping when he sees me between Lysander and Arden, and the mess I'm in. Seeing Grayson just makes me cry more, like seeing him releases the final dam on the emotions I've been trying to hold in. He walks over, picking me up out of Lysander and Arden, and hugging me tightly. "Ellelin, it's going to be okay."

"It's not," I whisper before Lysander tells him everything about Emrys. Only when he is done does Grayson make a sound. A growl, echoing deep from his chest, and it reminds me of a dragon roar. "Fuck Ares. Fuck the gods. I'm so fucking done with them." Grayson puts me on the bed. "Don't you fucking dare let them break you, Ellelin. You are the Queen of Ayiolyn and our mate. Wipe the tears away, rest and sleep, eat, and then we make a plan. The gods don't claim this world...you do with us at your side."

"Don't be a dick—"

I stop Arden. "No, Gray's right." I let out a frustrated sigh. Maybe I needed some tough love, because I need to find the fire in my chest, the one my grandmother and uncle taught me how to burn. "I am the granddaughter of a goddess, the daughter of a king of dragons, and the mate to five dragons. I am not weak, and I am not giving up. We'll get Emrys back and then kill Aphrodite."

"Murder is a plan I can get on board with," Lysander adds, and he makes my lips twitch.

Grayson kisses me softly. "One more battle. One last fight." I nod, wanting to believe it. It's always one more battle and one villain, one more injury and loss. I know I can't keep doing this. "The tsar is in the dungeons down below, with your mother watching him along with injured guards. She wants to come visit you when you're ready, but she thought you might need us first."

"Terrin's sister?"

"She is under the watch of the Shadow Dragons and Terrin…" Grayson rises to his feet. Arden picks me up and tucks me into the bed, making it clear where I'm staying. I'm not even strong enough to fight him off, despite Lysander healing me. "I've just heard something on the way up here. The Air Court is under attack. They're slaughtering them."

My blood goes cold. "How the fuck did you learn that?"

"Emrys's cousins and close friends got out in time with a bunch of children from the school…but they were the only survivors so far. I've ordered for portals to be sent but carefully, as we don't need Aphrodite getting in here again. We had to help as much as we can, but there's so many islands. Without the air king and the secrets of the Air Court, there's nothing we can do to get them all," Grayson softly explains, but I hear it in his voice, the same feeling echoing in my chest...horror. There are hundreds of thousands of people in the Air Court.

I push the cover back off my legs. "We have to go—"

"Fuck no." Arden covers me back up and shakes his head. "You're injured and weak."

"He's right," Lysander agrees. I must look like shit if Lysander is agreeing with Arden of all people. "I've healed you the best I can, but you need to rest. You need to sleep it off. You used an extreme amount of power and nearly died."

I huff. "No. Where's the sword? I'll get the sword, and I'll open a portal to—"

"No," all three of them say at the same time. Suddenly, having more than one insufferable mate doesn't seem like the best idea. Especially when they team up and use common sense.

Grayson sits next to me and picks up my hand. "I can't let you go there. Ares...well, Emrys, he'd be forced to kill you. You said that he nearly killed you before, and you wouldn't be able to defend yourself."

"We can't just leave the people of the Air Court to die!" I shake my head. "They are innocent."

"If we go in now, when we are all weak and injured…we are killing the best hope the rest of the world has. I don't want to leave them, but we cannot go in there right this moment," Arden gently explains. "Princess, they chose the Air Court for that very reason. It was easy to take and hard to defend. It's a really bad strategic move for us to go in, princess."

"I don't care about strategies. I want to go after Ares, and I can't just leave Emrys and his court to fall. I already had to leave him in the last test, and now he's been taken from me again! It's all my fault! He stepped in. He killed Ares for me. It should have been me." I suck in a breath. "And now I have to leave his people to die?"

"What would Emrys want?" Lysander asks. Shadows are pouring in around the room, and I barely notice them, notice my powers reacting to me. None of my mates move. They're not scared of it. Not the darkness in my soul. They never were. Emrys, least of all. My favourite moments of Emrys flash through my mind, every protective moment, every time he told me he loved me, every time I loved him too. "He'd want me to make a plan and attack with a strategy...not like this. We need to gather the armies, and we can do that. We can do it in a day. We just need time. Emrys, he wouldn't want me to risk my life. He wouldn't want us to risk you all." All the fight leaves me as I lie down, hearing them softly whisper to me that it will all be okay. It's hard to believe them.

I barely remember going to sleep. I must have passed out, and I don't dream. When I wake up, all I can smell is bacon and butter. Bacon sandwiches, to be exact, on a tray with juice and fruit, and a purple flower in a vase. Grayson is leaning against the window, looking out at the smoke that makes the daylight seem darker. Arden has his eyes closed as he sits on a plush chair in the corner of the room, scattered paperwork and scrolls on his lap, book piles pressed against the side of the seat. He isn't sleeping, I don't think, because he is so silent. Both of them have changed clothes and had a shower by the looks of it.

"Where's Lysander?" I ask. Arden nearly jumps from the sound of my voice, and I wince. Maybe he was sleeping.

Grayson turns, his eyes bloodshot, and he looks so tired it hurts my heart. "He's gone to help his brother with the healers. He's a good healer himself, and to save lives, he needed to leave." I raise an eyebrow. "Yes, surprisingly, he's grown a heart after becoming yours."

I grin just a little, but the smile leaves me the minute I think of Emrys. I clear my throat. "I'm feeling better now and—"

"I hate to interrupt your battle plan, but you're not leaving that bed until you have eaten." Arden points at the tray. "Try it, princess?"

I pout a little at him as he comes over, picking the tray up and dropping it in my lap, but the minute I take one bite of the sandwich, I end up devouring the lot. I was starving, and I barely noticed, but my mates did. I feel guilty even eating when Emrys is... My mother knocks the door twice as she steps into the door-frame of the open doorway. She looks as exhausted as everyone else, and there is a cut on her forehead, but she has changed clothes at least. She bows her head to Arden and Grayson before walking to the bed. "Darling, how are you feeling? I checked up on you, but you were sleeping earlier."

"Good," I tell her as she leans down and kisses my forehead.

"I saw you fighting out there, and you reminded me of your father…the last time I saw him." She gulps. "I couldn't save him, and I thought I wouldn't be able to…" She pauses. "I'm so happy to see you are okay, and I'm sorry about King Emrys."

"We will get him back," I firmly state, feeling certain that I will have Emrys back. I have a plan…and no one is going to like it. "I had—"

The door's knocked again, and a guard stands in the doorway, his head bowed low, and he doesn't rise. He is covered in blood, a massive wound on his stomach, and behind him is Jinks, barely managing to hold the man up as he passes out. Jinks half carries the man in, dropping him on the chair where Arden was with a grunt. "He just appeared in the middle of the castle, your majesties, and demanded to see you."

Arden leans down to lift the man's head up, and Grayson goes still. "It's Remy. He is a trusted royal guard and a friend of Grayson's."

"I barely recognised him with all the blood," Grayson claims, looking at Jinks. "Tell me you've called for a fucking healer?"

Lysander rushes in, heading to the man with only a quick glance my way. He heals him with water, the brilliant clear sea-like water washing the grime from Remy's face, and he finally wakes up. Grayson is in front of him but not close enough to touch. "What are you doing here? Where is my sister? You're her guard!"

"She's gone and you should kill me for my error." Grayson literally drains of colour, stumbling back. I climb out of the bed, rushing to his side.

Lysander swears. "What the fuck do you mean, gone? Dead or…?"

He gulps as the ground rattles under our feet and the castle walls groan, buckling under Grayson's magic. I know he isn't even aware he is doing it. A cold sweat covers his skin as I stroke his arm, wondering what is going on his head. The bond might be silent between us, but I can still feel him, feel the shock and devastation in his body. Remy nervously answers Lysander, who is still healing him. "She was dating someone, a young soldier, and I should have told you about that, but I didn't. She begged me not to, and I've never been able to say no to her. She snuck out in the night, and I realised she was gone a few hours later. We've searched everywhere for her, but then this came." He reaches into his pocket and pulls out a blood-soaked letter. A pink letter with silver writing above it. The air king. Grayson unfolds it as we all wait, and I read it with him.

Grayson loses it. The walls crack and the ground shakes like an earthquake, making people scream from below as the note falls from his hands. Vines stretch up every wall, cracking the stone as I move in front of Gray. Lysander picks the note up at my side and reads it out loud. "Come after me in the Air Court and your sister dies. Signed by Aphrodite."

Grayson's eyes are glowing green as he looks down at me, and my heart races, not in fear of him, but from the wrath of earth. The earth king, my precious mate, will destroy the world to get his sister back. I know because he would have destroyed it to get me back, too. I cup his cheek and make him look at me, even as I feel a tear fall over my hand from his eye. "We will save her. Together, Gray."

The earth king stares into my soul, in only the way a mate can. "I lost all of them but her. I promised to keep her safe, and she is just a kid. I can't lose—" He feels like he stops breathing as my heart breaks for him. We have to get her back. "If she touches my sister or you, the earth is going to crack open, and I'll take everyone with me. We will rule in the ruins."

"I'll help you destroy it," I vow. "But I have a plan, and it involves saving everyone."

CHAPTER 2

I stand in the entrance hall of my home, and my heart pounds in my chest as the castle walls groan in disapproval. This plan is stupid and insane, but at this point, I'll either do this or lose Emrys—and the chance of losing this entire world with him. The longer I leave them there stirring, the more risk they will attack us first, and we will lose in the state we are in right now. The courts are a mess thanks to Aphrodite invading each one, and the Air Court has fallen. I don't know how I'm going to tell Emrys that we couldn't save his court, his people, and there are only a few survivors. If he is still in there, in his body, which I have to believe he is, then he likely saw his own court get destroyed. How does he recover from that?

My mother stands at my side, and at the same time, Emrys's mother is upstairs crying her eyes out and has been crying since I told her everything that happened to Emrys. Her son. Her heir. I try to make a smile, but I don't feel it, not in my soul. I'm angry and so fucking done with the gods. I can't lose him.

"You look ready for war, darling, and I love seeing you strong like this but not when you're heartbroken and about to face an enemy who has defeated our family once before." She's right.

I smooth my hands down my tight clothes. We're both wearing all black, a silver crest of a crown with a dragon wrapped around it, clipped over my heart, right in the soft protective leather that goes from my neck to my ankles, its scale design reminding me of Grayson's dragon. She braided my hair, which I re-dyed all purple last night with Livia's help. Grayson hasn't slept and nothing I say to him is making it better, but his lips twitched when he saw my hair this morning.

"We are the strongest royals left in this world, and if we don't face them and try, then we are just as bad as they are. I am heartbroken, but I am angry. I'm angry enough that they should be scared," I tell my mother, my eyes softening. "I know they scare you, and you don't have to come with me. I understand and would never judge you for it."

She touches my arm. "Daughter, there isn't a fight I would not take for you. I fended off madness in a prison for years with just a dream of holding you one more time. You are my light and my reason to stand. I will fight with you; I wouldn't want to be anywhere else."

"I love you," I whisper, emotion threatening to overwhelm me. Just then, Lysander comes over, searching my face, but I reassure him. "I'm ready for this. You don't need to check. I'm okay."

Lysander arches a perfect eyebrow on his deliciously pretty face and smirks. "I know. I was admiring your outfit." Such a liar and he does it on purpose, knowing I'll smile. I want to make a joke, say something, but all I can see is Emrys literally choking me. Emrys…disappearing into himself. Lysander cups my face with his hands, no doubt feeling all of my emotions like they are his own. My mother walks away to Arden and Grayson to give us some time.

"The plan will work, and we will get him back," I insist.

"If we don't, help me destroy everything, my enemy?" My lips part. "I'll be the villain, and you can use me however you want as long as I'm with you." He rests his head against mine. "Say the word and we go in there and just start killing."

I gulp, knowing he would raise the sea and wash the world away for me. So much power, and yet it wouldn't save Emrys. I don't even know if he can be saved.

A roar outside, a dragon roar I know well, makes me look away. It's only been a few hours since we made a decision and a plan. Terrin listened to all of it, but he's still not spoken a word to me other than to see if I'm okay, and I hate leaving here while he is riddled with so much guilt it's choking to feel him through the bond. I know he is protecting me in his own way, but something feels different. "Let me come with you," Terrin finally speaks to me in my head.

Sighing, I look at the castle walls like I can

see through them and to my massive dragon flying in the rain outside. "I need you, but not when you're a dragon. I'm sorry, but there's little you can do in the Air Court. I need you to stay here and look after the people, our people."

"I hate being parted from you when you're about to go and do something dangerous and reckless." He growls.

"I thought that was why you fell in love with me. The continuously doing dangerous and reckless things, like riding a dragon, for example," I point out, needing to distract him.

It doesn't work. "It's my fault. All of it. I should have told you everything, and I didn't. When you get back, I need to tell you something that I didn't tell you before, but now that the tsar is here...well, I need to tell you."

I can hear the seriousness in his tone along with the guilt, but I'm confused about what he needs to tell me. "You know that your sister's decision to take a new rider wasn't your fault, or for him to bring the West army here. The war, it's not on you."

"We need to talk when you get back," he says with a finality that tells me this conversation is over. "And I love you. Be safe."

"I love you too," I whisper into his mind and feel him focus away from me. I get the sinking feeling Terrin has been keeping a big secret from me, and I need to know what it is. I trust him, completely, and I'm surprised.

I was so distracted that when I look back, Arden and Grayson have joined us. Each of my kings are ready for a fight, and I'm as turned on by their dark clothes, weapons and general look as I am terrified to lose them like Emrys. Arden kisses my forehead. "I'm glad that he can still speak to you, princess. You need someone in your overthinking mind."

"I miss all of you speaking to me like that." I turn to Grayson and focus. I know every second we don't go to the Air Court, it's tearing him apart as much as it is me.

Emrys. Please let there be something left for me to save. If he is really gone...I can't. Pain shoots through my heart as Grayson makes the portal and I think of my air king. He never deserved any of this. Lysander's hand is like a rock in the sea, making sure I don't drown in my own feelings as the Air Court spreads out in front of us. Angry, violent wind blows harsh and forgiving against the thrones and the broken archways that hang above this place. It's changed since I was last here. There has been more destruction, and it's almost like the air element has taken out its anger on the throne room. Even on this side of the portal, I can feel the icy breeze through the clothes I'm wearing. The sword seems to warm on my back just for a second, knowing that if I need it, that'll be my next move. It creeped me out on the battlefield, but I'm not holding it again unless everything hasn't gone to plan.

I have to believe in myself, in my kings and the plan we have, otherwise my legs would never move. We walk through together, my mother following after us. The wintry winds of the Air Court almost seem angry, bitter, but it doesn't match the pure wrath in my chest as I see Emrys sitting on a throne. It's not Emrys at all. His eyes are glaring red, burning, like I could see Ares's soul right there on the surface of his handsome face, smothering my beautiful mate's soul that is mine. He has always been mine.

Emrys is wearing all red, the colour washing out his tanned skin, only making his white hair look too pale, too much like death. Instead of

Emrys's green eyes I fell in love with, his are now red like Arden's but a darker shade like blood. I grit my teeth, tempted to rush over and plunge my sword straight through his chest to get Ares out. Even if it breaks me, that would be Emrys too. Ares, the smug bastard, smiles, knowing that I will not harm him. Ares wearing Emrys body is the perfect defence. Aphrodite saw the love between Emrys and me and set up the perfect way to keep them both alive. I wonder how many people they have done this with, how many hearts have felt like mine and been broken by the goddess of love and the god of war? If I don't stop them, will it ever end?

Aphrodite's lounging on the throne next to him in a long red dress. It's wrapped tight around her neck, and the silk falls around her curves. The bottom part sparkles like diamonds on the stone ground, and it matches her blood-red lips. She brushes her braided hair over her shoulder and smiles at me like we are long-lost friends. Every bit of hate, disgust and desire to kill her must be written all over my face, because she stops smiling for a second and looks away.

"You brought most of your lovers and

mother here to die a quick death? They should thank you, and it does save me chasing them down in each of those pesky courts." She makes a joke like this is all nothing to her. Maybe it isn't to her, I don't know, but she is ruining my life and joking about it.

I step away from Lysander and lift my head high. "Gods like to play games, so play one last game with me with the stakes higher than they have ever been." She rests her head on her bent arm and waves at me to continue. "You liked that I won your trials. I saw it. It was probably some sick but fun entertainment for you. It must get boring after all these years of being a god of love, trapped and married to him. Who better than the goddess of love to play with a girl that has five men in love with her? So, I offer you one more game. The winner gets this world and everyone in it. That includes my king, and Ares has to leave his body. I want Ayiolyn and I will claim it. Play or we can do the boring thing and fight until you are dead."

Her painted lips turn up into a huge smile, one that unsettles my stomach. "You're smart, smarter than your mother—"

My mother steps forward to my side.

"Careful how you speak about my daughter. I watched you, goddess of love, and I know you're nothing but a sad woman who is suffering, so you're going to bring the entire world down with you because you aren't happy."

Emrys…no, Ares speaks. "I'd like to trap her in a prison for years again. She clearly didn't use the time to learn how to shut her fucking mouth."

Aphrodite puts her hand on Ares's arm. Touching Emrys. Touching my mate. Burning jealousy makes the entire world darken around me, shadows slithering into gaps in the stone and waiting like snakes to strike at my command. Aphrodite doesn't move her hand, but she straightens. "The first thing my husband will do is kill Emrys's body and soul for good if you dare attack me in my home."

"This isn't your home," I snarl.

Grayson comes to my side, wrapping his arm around my waist. "Where's my sister?"

Aphrodite looks him up and down in a way I don't like. Fuck her. "Safe, below, in the dungeons, earth king. You're too pretty to see cry, so I won't kill her…yet. It's a bit cold, mind you. I might chuck her a blanket if you play nice. She cries all the time. She's rather annoying."

Grayson tenses and the ground cracks under our feet. "Give her back, you fucking—"

"Why would I do that? I'm not stupid. I realise exactly how powerful each of you is. My husband's in the air king's body and feels his power. He could suffocate this entire world if he wanted to. You could burn it down. You could drown it, and you, earth king, could rip the earth apart."

"If you touch a single hair on her head or she dies from the cold... If she has cried this entire time, ripping the earth apart would be the least of your problems. I'll help Ellelin rip you apart with her shadows and watch you scream. Trust my words. We will enjoy it." He cocks his head to the side. He isn't wrong. I've wanted her dead for so long, and every time I think there is a chance I could get time with my kings, something always goes wrong. My uncle Phobos once told me that murder doesn't count if they are annoying shitheads who deserve it, and I've kept that motto in my heart. "There won't be anything left of you to go to hell when we're done."

I see a flicker of fear in her eyes, and she purposely looks away from Grayson to me. "I do like games. It would be easier than attempting to kill you all. I want the world to worship me before I take on another, and this ultimate game, the last test, will be a warning to anyone that tries to revolt after I win. A legacy of the last royal dragons." She taps her fingers on the chair as the angry, stiff wind blows around my legs.

My mother suddenly disappears and my hand grabs for the empty space. "Where the fuck did you take her?" I scream, my shadows rising like pillars into the sky.

"Calm down," Aphrodite laughs. "I sent her down to the dungeons to keep that crying girl company and to add to the stakes."

I grit my teeth and look at Grayson, Arden and Lysander. One word and we fight until the death. My eyes drift back to Emrys, and the thought sinks in my chest. Even if we did win against Aphrodite, the last thing Ares would do is kill Emrys to spite me. Aphrodite carries on when I look back at her. "Here is my deal. Four tests, one for each of you to complete and win. You need to win three out of four, and if we draw, I win. One of you will have to come back each day. If you win, then I will leave this world. I will take Ares's soul with me and leave Emrys's body here for you to sort out. Alive, of course. I will not hurt anyone, and I will leave the princess and your mother here, too. Unharmed."

"You leave this world with no powers. You lose everything, including your magic," I add in before she can continue. "If I'm risking everything, so are you. Unless you're frightened."

Taunting her is easy. She laughs, but Ares isn't impressed. "Fucking hell, do not make that deal for a stupid game. It isn't worth—"

"Deal," Aphrodite interrupts Ares, who slumps back in his seat, looking pale. Emrys looks sick and I hope it's because Emrys's soul is fighting in there, making it hell for Ares. "But if you lose, I'm going to take over with four dragon kings at my side, the four elements, and they will be tasked with killing you in front of everyone." My mates blanch and my heart races. I stare at my mates, wishing that we could talk in our minds to each other. But I don't need to do that to know that we can't go back now. Our decision was set before we came here.

"You have a deal."

"Good. Water king, your test is first. Come tomorrow, at dawn, alone. Anyone that comes with you is dead," Aphrodite demands. "And I vow to abide by the rules set today and promise safety in and out of the tests. I vow it on my blood." She touches her neck, running a nail across it. Her blood freely flows down her pale neck.

"I make the vow too." Lysander unclips a blue shimmering dagger from inside his cloak and quickly cuts his hand. Each of my kings makes the deal until I am left. The blood of my mates drips off the dagger like a warning as I slide it across my own palm. I vow to any gods that are listening. Let this be a warning of what happens when gods come to our world. I twist the dagger around and point it right at Aphrodite. "You are going to be a warning that haunts all the gods that are scattered across the worlds. This is what happens when you come to a world that is not yours and you try to mess with the rulers. When you're dead, this final game is going to be our legacy. Not yours."

Her eyes flicker with something, something I can't read, but I look one more time at Emrys with my heart, feeling like it's in his hands, being crushed, before nodding to Gray. Grayson opens a portal right behind us, and I take his hand as we walk back through. When it closes, my heart doesn't feel like it came through, and it will be lost with Emrys and my mother in the Air Court until this game is over.

"Granddaughter." I spin around to see my grandmother and Cronus standing in the centre of the room.

"How?" I splutter, unable to get any other words out, but my grandmother opens her arms.

"Your family is here and you're not fighting for this world alone. Now tell me, where is my daughter?"

CHAPTER 3

ARTEMIS

"*D*id you hear what Elle and the kings did with your mother?" Kian questions before letting out a sigh. "It's chaos down there, with her grandmother just appearing along with a dead army. I was happy to escape up here even before you found me."

I nod. It's exactly why I came in here, to find him. I needed him, and I needed my mind off the madness of the castle and the haunting knowledge it's my parents causing all of this. Just for a second, I can be with the man I love and imagine the world isn't falling apart outside of this room. If Elle and the kings lose, we're going to lose everything good in this world. I won't live in this world with my parents ruling, and I know for certain the first person they will go after is Kian because I love him. My mother will revel in torturing him, breaking his soul, right along with mine. I believe in Elle; I believe in the kings and their strength. I feel somewhere deep in my soul that good always wins...but what about the people in the grey? "I know we should be down there offering advice or doing anything to help, but I can't. Something doesn't feel right to me."

"Because they're your parents?" he softly questions. He's lying on his side, elbow bent and his head propped up in his hand. He is completely naked, except for the blanket covering his waist, and he is so pretty it hurts to stare for too long. Even now, knowing exactly what my parents are, he is offering me a moment to grieve for the parents they could have been with no judgment. He never judges me, and sometimes I wonder what I did to deserve him.

"No, they are already dead to me. I don't hold love for them anymore, and I'm learning slowly that I likely never did. It's more than that. Every night, I'm haunted by the same dream." *Dream* is a light word for it. The feeling I get, the peace like nothing could ever touch me, is what makes the dream feel so alive.

"What's your dream?"

I turn on my side to face him and his question, the sheet falling down my back. His eyes drag downward with a burning heat that is in direct contrast with the cool, calm personality he has. He reaches forward and tucks some curls of my hair behind my ear. They only bounce back of course, but it makes Kian smile, the way he only smiles at me.

I clear my throat. "It's weird."

"Tell me." His soft demand brushes against me. He touches my nose gently. "No secrets, no barriers between us."

Our promises to each other. Our vows written only in our words, spoken under bedsheets in the dead of the night. I trust him, even with the ugly things like my dreams. "We're swimming, me and you, but the lake is black and red. Not like blood or dirt, but a beautiful glittering shade of vibrant red like fire and black like death. We're laughing and splashing water on each other. We look so happy. Not older than we are now, but just happy. This dream just keeps coming back again and again to me, and it always feels so strange, not like a normal dream."

The dreams began when I really got a hold on using my magic and the training I've had. I'm not great, not by any means, but I think I can use my power to defend myself. I can take energy, power, from another person, and I only need to touch them for it to work. Kian thinks I've only touched an inch of my true power and reminds me I'm the daughter of two powerful gods, and it makes me a god, too. A title I never wanted but will use to protect my friends. My true family.

"I can take you swimming anytime, but I am unaware where there is a black and red lake." He sighs. "Dreams with water are sacred in my family. It's said when a royal has a dream about water, it is a prophecy."

"Do you think because we are together, and I take your energy, your power, by accident most days...I could be seeing your dream?" I nervously question.

"If you are, I look forward to swimming with you in this strange place. I don't care as long as I am with you." He kisses me softly. "I have to leave. I'm on healer duty for tonight. But I can take it off if you need me. I know you must be scared of all the changes in the castle and a dead army outside."

"I'm not scared of them." I rest my head on his shoulder. "Well, they are creepy to look at, but I'm more concerned with my parents and their plans. If they kill Grayson's sister, if my father doesn't let go of Emrys's body...and what if Emrys is gone? I can't live—"

"I won't let anything happen to you." He cups my cheek and turns my tear-soaked eyes to his. "I am in love with you and the good heart you bury deep in your chest. I have loved you since I first met the real you down in those dungeons, when I saw that you were so fucking confused and trapped by family guilt that you couldn't breathe let alone make choices for yourself. But I knew then, or suspected at least, that I wanted you forever. You are so brave, so brilliant, and I know you will never forgive yourself for your own past actions, but I think you should. I want you to marry me. Be my mate, my wife. Every binding term there is known to all the gods. Just be mine."

"I've always been yours, and yes to every

single binding term," I whisper. "I loved you too, you know. The moment you told me that story of the whale, when we were never really speaking about the whale, were we? It was… I always thought myself a villain in the story. I didn't deserve a happy ending. But I will spend the rest of my life trying to get out of the dark, even if it's just into the grey, so that I can be with you."

He kisses me so deeply and brands me with each moment. He groans when bells ring across the castle, the magic castle telling Kian his shift has begun. "I'll work and then meet you after to tell everybody about us. I want to shout it from the castle top."

My cheeks burn. "Alright, I'll try not to hide behind you when they stare."

He shakes his head at me. "They will hug and congratulate us. They are our family." He's right and there isn't a day that will pass that I don't wonder if I deserve it. I watch as he gets dressed in a tunic marking him as a healer from the Water Court, his hair still messy as he kisses me one more time and leaves our room. I go into the bathroom, flip the shower on, and stare at myself in the mirror. The steam slowly fills the room like a fog over the horizon, and the door slams shut with a bang, right before I feel the magic in the air. When I turn around, my mother's right in front of me. She's dressed in a red suit, her long hair braided down the back of her neck. She's standing by the door, the fog flowing around her.

My mouth parts and my hands shake. I slide them behind my back so she doesn't see. She would always comment on how strong women don't shake and how it's a sign of weakness. I know that isn't true. "How are you here—and don't bother answering, just leave."

Her mouth widens into a smile that reminds me of a cat from a story book that was read to me as a kid. The picture of the striped cat used to scare me even then. "You can appear to your blood, call to them, travel to them, even at any time, if you're strong. You're not. I could come and get you right now if that's what I wanted."

"No." I end up whimpering, even if I want to shout and scream.

She laughs into my face. The way she's always laughed *at* me, not *with* me. "Has your first love tempered your mind against us so quickly? I'm disappointed with you for choosing their side. This world's going to fall and soon. I'm going to be forced to kill so many, and I thought you'd happily serve at my side. I'll make another heir, maybe one for each court when I have all the kings. But you were my firstborn. You may not have any power, but you are still my child."

Screaming you're a mother doesn't make you worthy of the title. "Have you suddenly grown love and affection for me, or is it some more pretence, because I don't actually believe you. Giving birth to someone doesn't make them love you if you constantly abuse them."

My mother shakes her head at me, more than once, her complicated braid falling over her shoulder. She never braided my hair, no, she always wouldn't because she knew I didn't like my hair in my face, and I asked her so many times. The braid is a silly thing to focus on, but it reminds me of all the ways she failed me. All the times I begged for attention and love, and she gave me nothing. I think the only thing she ever gave me was my name. She was never a mother to me. Still, she wants me back now to use me. I'm another soldier to her and nothing more. "Come back and things will be better. I prom—"

My body may show how scared I am, but I hold my head high. "No. I will never come back to your side. If this world falls, then I fall with it and my real family."

She sighs like I'm an inconvenience. I don't know what she expected from me, but I get the impression she expected me to come with her. "Do you like being with them so much, or is it just that you're upset over me killing your servant? I'll get you another one. I've just spent the better part of my day making an underwater maze for the water king to die or fail in. I'm tired and in no mood to chase you, so change your mind, cut your hand, and ask for me to be here. The magic will do the rest."

I will be telling Elle and Lysander everything she just accidentally told me. Maybe something good can come from her being here, even if it hurts to see her. "She wasn't just a servant!" I shout at her. "She was the one who sang me lullabies and held me when I cried. She was the one who made me my favourite foods, who sat with me and told me about human culture in a fun way. She was the one who told me I did not need to be what you trained me to be because you never mothered me. You trained me to become your soldier, to become a betrayer, and how to hurt someone, but it never felt right to me to do it, and I wish I'd listened to myself, to my own instincts, and I didn't. I failed myself, but I'm never doing that again. I am loyal to the Spirit Court and its queen. I am loyal to the dragons, not the gods. I do not want you here. So, fuck off back wherever you came from, Mother. I will pray to any powerful entity that will listen, anybody that will give us even an ounce of luck, that she kills you and is done with the fucking goddess of love who knows nothing about love."

Her eyes sharpen. Sharpen the way that I'm used to when she attacks me, but I realise she can't. Without the staff or my blood and magic, she doesn't have enough power to get to me. I open the door, letting the steam fall out. "I'm so disappointed in you. You'll never be loved, you know. Not in the way you desperately want to be. You are unlovable."

I think of Kian. All her lies, everything she's told me a hundred times, none of it is true. For some reason, it gives me closure. Closure on my childhood, closure on everything. To know in this moment right now that it's not true. I ignore her, knowing it will drive her insane, and I walk out. I leave her in the shadows of the fog in the past, as my future is with a Water Court prince who taught the daughter of the goddess of love what love truly is.

CHAPTER 4

"They're creepy lovestruck puppies, and I can't mentally get my head around the fact they are ancient gods."

Hope's long dark hair catches in the wind and blows around her face. She pushes it away and leans on the stone wall barrier. Trying not to laugh, I join her and look over the lands around the castle, and for a moment I don't see the burnt ground, the ruins of the war that just happened, or the graves dug a few miles out for all the dead. I don't see the fires burning the bodies of the dragons we lost and our enemies we killed. I just see the day I rode on Arden's back and flew with the dragons who would become my mates, around the land I didn't know was my home. Not yet. It was the first moment I felt like I didn't want to leave this world. The memory crumbles as reality pushes down on my senses with the smoky smell and the icy wind. The rising sunlight makes the sky look pink at the moment, like a Barbie doll designed the sky. I doubt Hope even knows what one is.

"You wouldn't want to know what I walked in on only ten minutes ago. I got up early because sleep just wasn't happening for me, and it turns out they both decided a naked bathtub with their dead army people fanning them was a perfect thing to do in the middle of the dinner hall," I mutter, wishing I could burn it from my memory. They were covered up by the water, but still. I think my grandmother is keeping Cronus distracted, and it's for the best. I honestly thought Cronus was going to kill Aphrodite and Ares because the news of my mother made my grandmother cry. I don't trust the unfeeling bastard, but I trust my grandmother and she loves him. I want him to take Aphrodite out too, just like I told him yesterday, but I can't. No one can do that because the consequence of that move is losing Emrys.

Hope bursts into laughter and I let myself laugh with her, let my shoulders drop and the world's problems fade for a moment. Only when our laughter stops, when the dragons fly across the sky like a dark shadow and I watch them, does Hope bring it up. "I'm sorry about Emrys. I love him too, not like you do, but like a brother. I know he would tell me to make you give up on this if it risks your life and the kings'. He wouldn't want you to die for him."

"I know," I bitterly whisper. If it was the other way around, I'd beg him not to do what the kings and I have signed ourselves up for. "But he's in there. He looked so pale, and Ares struggled and looked tired. If he struggled to even hold a conversation up for long, something isn't going to plan. So I think Emrys is in there fighting, and we'll fight for him. Starting with Lysander today." I watched the army spread out far and wide, all dead but standing corpses of bone so white they glitter in the light. "If I lose him...I don't think there will be anyone who could stop the darkness that would explode out of me and drown every world."

"You sound like a goddess." Hope looks to the sky. "And what says you aren't one? You are so powerful, and isn't that all gods are? Powerful people who can change the world?"

A goddess. I guess it does run in my blood. "Then gods can be killed. I will end them both." A dragon roar is our only warning before Hope's dragon swoops up in front of us, the scales of her belly so close I could reach out and touch them. I haven't had time to talk with Terrin other than checking in. It's been too crazy since my grandmother got here. She kept us up talking late last night, making battle plans, organising everything until I absolutely felt exhausted. I barely remember Arden practically picking me up and carrying me back to our room before I fell asleep. I woke up before he did. Grayson was training already, a sweaty mess beating up some of the earth guards who came through to protect him, and I narrowly avoided that mess, so I didn't have to do any training. I'll train with him when he has calmed down; otherwise, my muscles will never survive. I don't know where Lysander is, but part of me is worried about seeing him because I might ask him not to go into that test where he might not come out of it.

"You look like a thousand things are going

on in your mind right now." Hope's voice cuts through my thoughts.

I clear my throat. "Distract me. Please." She opens her arms. "What about Xandry? Things are weird between you two since we've come back from that world. What happened out there?"

She clears her throat, looking extremely uncomfortable. It's good, it's something else to focus on. I doubt she will tell me anything, but when she looks away from me to the sun, she tells me everything about how uncomfortable she is sharing this. "We're both from that world. He followed me through."

I wasn't expecting that. "Why would he do that?"

"Because I'm his mate and I'm a wolf shifter and so is he, but he's an alpha. Essentially means that he can control a pack, do whatever he likes, and in the same way that mates work in this world, it's the same for the world I'm from. The alpha was my brother, is my brother. I found out answers to my family and what happened. I was sent here because I'm an alpha female and powerful. Back then, it was dangerous for people like me."

"Hope." I touch her arm. "Why didn't you stay?"

"Despite everything going wrong here, this world is my choice and my home. I looked for my family for my entire life, like it could give me some kind of closure on wanting something more, but the truth was, when I found it, I actually didn't want it." She sighs. "I know that sounds mad, but it's true."

"I wanted to go back to Earth so much that I was blocking out all the reasons that I'd found to stay in this world. When I was back on Earth, with a chance to just stay there and live a normal life, have everything that I'd asked for—what they'd given me on a plate—I didn't want it. I desperately wanted the life that I already had and chose for myself. I came back here to fight for this world, and I wouldn't ever willingly leave. It's my home and I understand why you didn't stay there." I cock my head to the side. "So, the sexy tutor, he's your mate? I always thought there was something between you two, but I didn't want to be pushy."

She snorts in laughter for a second. "He chose a religion that makes sure that he can't have sex or take a mate so he didn't have to watch me with Lysander. I chose Lysander because he saved me, but I actually wanted Xandry first, but he was my only real friend and I didn't want to risk him rejecting me, so I took an easier path. I think he now thinks I rejected him. It's all a mess. Oh gods, my love life is messier than yours." I really try hard not to laugh because she is sort of right. It's messy but it sounds like a conversation could solve so many of their problems.

My efforts to not look amused fail, and we both burst out laughing together. "I'm pretty sure it's loads of girls' fantasies to tame a priest, so you should go and do that." I wipe away my tears of laughter and get serious for a second. "He's right there, Hope. He's gorgeous and, from the little I know of him, brave enough to follow you through to another world and then back."

"I know. I think I'm scared to tell him how I feel, and I'm rarely scared of anything." She turns to me. "I'm going to the Water Court. Lysander and Kian asked me to escort their mum back with Xandry and secure the court. Make them aware their king is back and pissed off."

I wince. "That will be dangerous. You don't have to—"

"You're not the only one who wants to defend her home. The Water Court is fucked up, but it's my home and I need to try to fix it. I'll be okay," she promises.

"I know you're not a hugger, but this once. Don't stab me." I wrap my arms around her tightly before she can run away. Surprisingly, she hugs me back, but it's a quick hug as she pulls away, leaning her hip on the wall. I leave her to it, knowing it's time I found Lysander before he leaves.

"You're my best friend, you know. Just in case you die before I see you next. Don't fucking haunt me."

"You're on the top of my list, bestie," I say, winking at her, and she laughs as I slip back into the castle. I'm not even joking. I have a list, and pissing her off by haunting her is definitely how I'll keep myself amused. Not that I plan on dying anytime soon. I walk back to the castle, down through the rooms, touching the walls as I go to say hello to my magical castle friend. I go back to our rooms, looking for Lysander, but instead I find the matron alone on the couch by the fire. "Hello."

"Princess." She bows her head low and stands up, her black cloak pooling at her feet. "Has he told you yet?"

"Who told me what?" I question.

She taps her stick on the stone as she walks to me and then straight past me to the door. "Not yet, then. I will find you again, princess." She vanishes into thin air, leaving me staring at the space she was in and wondering if she meant Terrin. The matron is scary in a way I can't explain, and the thought of her coming back to see me doesn't settle well. The castle clearly puts up with her, and she can't be a threat if the castle is okay with her around. It's too protective.

I head back out of the rooms and trust my senses to search for my king. I may not be able to speak in my mind to him, but I can find him. He's my mate. I'm surprised when I find myself getting lower and lower in the castle until I come to the once guarded doors, where no guards stand. Lysander stands before the dark doors, black leather scaled armour covering him from his neck to his dark, heavy boots. "Don't tell me you're going in there."

"Do you think I'd do that alone, spirit witch?" he murmurs, turning to fully face me. I smile at his frown, at the serious set of his eyebrows. "I was thinking of a way to block this off so you don't go in there without me to protect you. It's driving me fucking insane thinking I might not—"

"Don't you fucking say what I think you are about to," I snarl, anger rising like a storm in my blood. "I won't go in there, and you'll know that because you're going to win and come back. You're Lysander, the fucking king of the water and sea and everything in the Water Court. You. Don't. Lose. Promise me. You can't die."

He closes the space between us, slipping his hand around the back of my neck, sinking his fingers into my hair, searching my eyes, knowing that only he can make me feel this way. Loving Lysander is like loving the sea itself, like sinking in a force of nature that no one can control, and he only wants me. "The last thing I'd do is drown this world and leave only you left. For the record between us, death may try to part us one day, but I'm a stubborn fucker and I'm holding onto you."

My heart races. "I'm not letting go either. Fight for me. Come back. I would like it if you left my other mates alive with us if you decide to drown the world. I'm kind of partial to them."

He shrugs. "I don't give a fuck."

I hit his shoulder, but he catches my hand, twisting and pinning it behind my back before crushing his lips down on mine, kissing me deeply and branding me as his. He doesn't need to, I'm hopelessly his already. Time fades into just numbers with Lysander, like there is no beginning or end to the clock. Soon, I'm breathless and panting. Only then does he let me go. "I'll come back; I'll win and then sink my cock into you for my prize."

Heat trickles down my spine as he lets me go, and I want to grab him, lock him away so there isn't a chance of losing one of my mates. Is this how they felt as I did dangerous things over and over to save them? The darkness behind me seems to whisper in my ear as he walks up the steps, clicking his fingers and a portal opening. The song of the fifth court plays for Lysander, and if that isn't welcoming him as a future king consort to me, I don't know what is. Lysander looks over his shoulder once, right before plunging into the court of our enemies.

CHAPTER 5

KING LYSANDER

*T*hank fuck I can swim, because the love goddess bitch has flooded the portal. I step straight into a current fast enough to take any air left in my body and rip it straight out. The current sends me in a spiral, down what feels like a spinning tunnel of seawater, the salt stinging my eyes before I manage to swim towards the edge, grappling on to a stone ledge. I pull myself up with sheer strength and manage to stand, glaring at the blinking of the bright yellow light that hangs right above me.

The river I just climbed out of is laced with the smell of the Water Court, and as I lean down, dipping my fingers into the current, I feel my home. I'm in my court, deep below the violent oceans where no king has ventured. I didn't make a portal to come here, yet somehow she has twisted even that. Getting my eyes on Emrys was my first plan so I could look my mate in the eye and tell her he is still alive. She needs to hear that and, fuck it, I want to see him too. I'd never admit it to his face, but he is my brother in every way but blood, and fuck am I going to let him die. The clear water is spinning round in a circle going deep, likely to where the test begins, gathering by the lights down at the bottom that look like a threat.

"Back to it." Reluctantly, I dive straight back in, sucking in air before letting the water take me. I can hold my breath longer than anybody else in this world. The water itself bends to me, to my control, making the pull of it easier on my body, not like it's ripping me apart as it would anyone else. Fuck her. Bringing me to my court and playing games? The bitch is going to die.

I casually allow the water to glide me all the way down until eventually I fall straight out through a waterfall and dive straight down into a massive, deep pond. I swim to the top and walk forward, using the water to propel me with little effort. It's not too deep, easy enough for me to stand on and walk out after a minute of swimming. I'm soaking wet with the cold water, but the water is relaxing for me, the only place I feel like I can be myself. It's my power. It's my soul and what echoes through my blood.

Aphrodite stands at the edge of the lake, in a mocking blue princess gown with Water Court symbols all over the skirt. She has a crown on her head, crystal blue spikes stretching higher than the size of her head, and it looks similar to the one my mother wears for formal occasions. I want to rip it straight off her head, along with half of her stupid hair, and stab it into her heart until she bleeds. "Welcome, water king. I thought an entrance like this would be suitable for you."

I growl. "You spelled the portal I made."

"Of course I did. This is your court. Part of it that is on the outskirts. I don't want to get you too close to your own home." She looks like I should thank her.

"I'm aware of what my lands are, you fucking bitch. I don't want small talk, so let's get fucking on with it before I get bored and murder you for sport. Fuck what your deranged husband does," I snarl at her. I'm bluffing. I wouldn't risk Emrys, Elle's mother, and Grayson's sister by losing my temper. I'm playing this game for my mate and the dream of fucking her every day of the week and not having enemies looming over our heads, other worlds to get lost in, or any other shit that interrupts me being inside my mate.

"Straight to the point, and a brute about this all. It's why I picked you first. You're not the fun one to play with now you're not being the villain anymore."

I bare my teeth at her. "Come near my mate again, bitch, and I'll happily slip back into the man who doesn't give a fuck about destroying the world."

"I might be the goddess of it, but love like you feel makes you weak." She rolls her eyes at me. "I won't tell you much, as you've been so rude. All the tests your kind has done with the humans over the years. There's plenty to look through to find ideas for my last games. It was easy to find something you might not survive so easily. Your father's test for your mother, for example, was interesting."

A maze, just like Artemis warned Elle about.

My father's water test was particularly brutal, and no one, unless they are favoured by water, would win it. My mother is loved by the water element, and she often told me the story of how when I was born, the water rose a high tide to flood her birthing chamber and be the first thing to greet me in this world. I was born in water, and in it, nothing can stop me. I struggle to remember what happened in the maze my mother faced, only that it was underwater with tiny pockets of air here and there. The aim of it was to press a series of buttons before getting to the middle.

I grit my teeth as she points to the wall, ordering me like a dog with a pointed command. I'm not interested in being in her company more than I have to, so I take it. Winning this is all that matters. I don't bother looking back at her either. "Oh, water king." I stop. "I won't let you die in there, maybe come close to it. But you have twenty-five minutes to the dot to find the middle of the maze. If in twenty-five minutes, you are not there, you don't return to your queen and you are thoroughly under my spell forever."

I look at her, the dead goddess still walking but not for long, as I make a vow. "So, in exactly twenty-four minutes and fifty-nine seconds, I'll make sure I'm dead long before you get to touch me."

She looks pissed off, just like I wanted before leaving her to go straight through the door. It slams shut behind me. Just as I expected, water rushes at me, but I hold my hand up, calming the waves until they smother my body but at my pace. The walls themselves are shimmery, veils of controlled water, with balls of light inside that look like tiny creatures, making everything glow in a soft green haze. I swim forward, searching for the first air pocket, letting the water direct me on my path. First right, then the left, before I come up in the water pocket just above. I swim up and suck in a breath of fresh air before rolling my shoulders of any tension. This will be easy.

I dive back down, only to come face to face with a Dartle. I barely miss the snap of its jaws, but one of its sharp teeth drags down my arm, leaving a wide-open cut, and my blood pools into the water, leaving a sickly metallic taste in my mouth. I groan in pain, only making me inhale water into my lungs and it fucking burns. I turn the water to ice in my hands, making a spear, and spin round to face the Dartle. It slams at me again, this time smashing me against the wall. My spear snaps against its skin, doing nothing to touch it and the wrap of red magic protecting it. Fucking Aphrodite. I reach for my daggers on my belt and find them all gone. Fucking Aphrodite again.

The Dartle turns around. The big lugging creature takes a while to make the corner. It looks like an eel, except its mouth makes up pretty much all of its body. It's got rows of glittering silver teeth and huge scaled eyes to match. The disgusting creatures, which have pretty much been wiped out of the seas of the Water Court due to the fact they have no brains, don't listen to my family's command, and they eat everything like they are starving beasts twenty-four seven. Some surviving Dartles have been buried deep down below in the dark waters of the north where no one wishes to go. I should have hunted them years ago. They're deadly. These ones seem impenetrable, but everything can die, especially in my element.

My dragon roars in my mind, wanting to come out, but it's too big in this maze and we'd get trapped. I hope there's only fucking one down here, but I doubt it. Everything got a lot more dangerous real fucking quick. I think of Elle. I think of my beautiful, sexy and smart mate. This is for her, and there is absolutely nothing I wouldn't do for her. I'd die for her without questioning why. She was never my enemy. That was a joke. A joke because I was once told to keep your enemies closer than your friends. I knew if I called her my enemy, I'd be able to keep her as close as I fucking wanted without admitting I was in love with her from the first moment I met her. I'm not dying in this. I'm not going to die. I'm going back. I'm going to prove to Elle, prove to everyone, I am the water king. There's nothing in the water, the seas, that can stop me.

I let my power flood through my veins. I let the core of the sea demand my soul as I stare at this creature that I know damn well will not listen to its king. It doesn't have the brain power to understand my command, to understand what it is facing. I swim fast, using the water to propel me as I search for the switch and leave the Dartle to chase me. I come across so many dead ends, feeling eyes on me, but the Dartle is soon lost behind in the tight spaces in the walls.

My lungs start to burn, and I realise it must have been ten minutes at least. I think I can hold my breath for about twenty minutes, which gives me a good indication of how much time I have left.

I finally find the first switch on the wall. It's hidden around a corner I hadn't seen. I slam my hand through the wall, pressing the red glowing button, and the wall behind me disappears. Beautiful little green creatures swim around my body like a wave. This time, I expect it when one more of those things comes flying at me through the creatures, eating them as it goes. The big Dartle nearly takes my entire arm off. But I grab its mouth, using all the force I have to fling it as I fly through the gap and go quickly into the new area.

I spin around and by sheer damn luck— maybe there's a god watching me—I find another button straight away down the first corridor I check. I press it, and the wall disappears to the right. This time, there's no monster behind it to eat the creatures and me. For at least three minutes, I keep getting trapped by several dead ends before I finally find an air pocket and swim up. I suck in the air, only allowing myself a second of my head above the water because I don't trust what's underneath it, before diving back down.

Elle. Elle. Elle. I think of her; I think of my spirit witch. Like she's right here next to me, but I'm so fucking glad she's not. Her long, divinely soft lavender hair and her piercing blue eyes that look like the colour of the sea outside my throne room, which I've stared at for so many hours on end I've lost track. Elle, with her curves and skin so soft, I could kiss her forever and still be desperate for one more kiss. Elle, who is my soulmate and forgave me when I never deserved it. I will deserve her now.

I dive around the corner, and I finally spot the centre of the maze. In the centre, there's a giant red button to press, but around it, there's at least thirty giant Dartles, and each one of them turns towards me. Fear slams into my chest as I realise that this is a lot of them to take on. I pull all the power I can to control the water like a barrier and stop them. They slam into it like a wave, pushing against my power with all their force. I grit my teeth, digging my feet into the sandy ground to hold them back, holding my arms out in front of me.

I roar under the water, knowing I'm not going to die this way, as I can't hold them back and I can't kill the fuckers. I'm going back to my mate. I'm going back to the Spirit Court, to my home, which is her. It's always been her. I grab onto power, pushing past the limits that I've always had in place. Pushing past everything. My dragon snarls from inside me, tearing at the edges to get out and to trust it. I let my dragon take over. Let it transform out of my body in a burst of blue scales and icy fire. He slams onto the sandy floor just as the Dartles all slam into us.

We roar loud enough for the stars to hear, knocking off the Dartles who sink their teeth into us over and over. Icy fire bursts out of my dragon's mouth and in a path, freezing and destroying the enemies around us for the most part. It's an endless fight. Freezing and ripping them apart is painful and tiring. My dragon roars and snarls, using its claws and teeth to devour them. Time seems like it never ends until only silence and the decay of bodies is left and my dragon bleeding into the water.

My dragon, tired and done, whines as it lies down in the sand. I force him to shift back, panicking as red fills the water around me, as I look at the dozens of bite marks on my body and noting I've lost enough blood to feel dizzy and sick. I slap my cheek. "Wake the fuck up. Elle needs us."

Just saying her name out loud is enough to make my legs move and for my mind to block out the pain. With her on my mind, I keep moving towards the button, so close. Just as I reach my hand out, something slams into me hard enough to send me spinning across the water, and pain blinds me as I thump into the sand. The Dartle's mouth wraps around my stomach and legs, pushing me into the sand as its teeth rip through my body, and I'm fucking powerless. I'm dead. I'm dying. No, fucking NO! Pain forces me to shout and scream as I slam my fists onto its face to get it the fuck off me, but it digs in more. It's ripping me apart.

Time seems to freeze just for a moment. The water stills in an unnatural way and so does the Dartle. I look up to see a man floating in the water, and he is something more than a man. A ghost. He looks ethereal, hovering with a crown in his hands, a blue sparkling crown, with a water symbol dead in the centre. "Who are you?"

The water swirls around his glowing body like it's part of him. "My name is Poseidon, and my brother allowed me this one trip to stop your death in honour of the queen of death. You are my descendant, King Lysander, as are all the kings of the Water Court." Behind him, hundreds of ghost outlines hover like a wave. I can't quite see all of them, but I know every royal that's ever existed, including my father, is here to help me. My family came.

My eyes lock on Poseidon as he comes down, floating next to me as he places a crown on my head. Power floods through my system and I feel everything. I feel every wave of the sea, every creature in the waves, and every storm hovering on the horizon. I feel the water like I am a part of it in a way I never have before. My entire body glows dark blue when I open my eyes, and flames made of ice float around me in the water. "This is a crown made for you by your father, kept in the court of spirit until the time was right. The sea answers to you, as do all its creatures. It cannot kill its king.

Command it and change the future, King Lysander."

He fades away, and time begins again. But everything has changed. I punch the Dartle with a hand full of icy fire, and it splits right down the middle before blasting into blue flames that disappear as soon as they appeared. The water stills for me, and I look around, seeing dozens of surviving Dartles watching from the edges. "Don't fucking try it. I am your king, and if you live in my sea, you bow to me."

They listen. The sea itself listens, moving around me as I walk straight to the button and slam my hand on it. The water drains away, leaving the last of the Dartles flopping on the ground as they slowly die. A portal appears right in front of me, Aphrodite's voice filling my head. "Well done." She doesn't mean it and I fucking love that she isn't happy. "Tell the fire king it's his day tomorrow and to bring the princess too."

I want to tell her to fuck off, but I know I can't. I look up, like I can see her, hoping she can see. "Get the fuck out of my court before I drown you, goddess. You are not welcome." I walk through the portal, right out into the bedroom where Elle is pacing up and down at the end of the bed.

I instantly smile when I see her. She has that effect on me, the ability to make everything seem fine in the world by just being in the same room. She's gnawing on one of her nails, and she doesn't notice me straight away. When she looks up, her eyes widen. "Lysander!" she shouts my name before running my way. She crashes into me as the portal snaps shut at my back. "God, you're bleeding! You're bleeding everywhere!"

"I'm fine." I pick her up and kiss her. I can heal, and I do. It doesn't take much water, just the water around me to heal everything. It feels effortless as I send the water around to fix my body. Elle's eyes flicker to my crown, and she frowns.

"How did you—" I don't stop kissing her as I lead her back to the bed, and I don't give her time to ask anything yet.

"I won and the rest I can tell you later," I explain between kisses, moving down to her neck until she moans when I kiss a spot that she loves. "I want what was promised." Her eyes darken. Fuck, I need to taste her first. I pick her up and carry her to our bed, watching as she lies down before me like a fucking treat I want to sink my teeth into and fuck until we are both hoarse. I run my hand down her jaw, past her parted lips, and to her neck. I'm holding that neck as I fuck her.

But for now, I bite my own lip as I run my hand over her breast, her pebbled nipple touching my palm, and she gasps loudly. I grin to myself, gripping her leggings and dragging them down her thighs and legs until I chuck them away. I rip her top off until her perky tits are mine to see, and I take my time rubbing my thumbs across the hard peeks until she is wriggling her ass for more. The sweet smell between her legs calls to me, and I kneel, pulling her ass to the edge of the bed before sinking my face in between her legs. Learning what sets Elle off has been my greatest learning experience, and making her come is fucking art work to me.

Her moan is music to my ears, and her back arches off the bed. Fuck. My cock presses against my trousers painfully, begging me to let him out to fuck her. But my cock can wait. I'm tasting her and enjoying myself. I'm making her come with my tongue first. I flick her clit with my tongue until she is begging me, digging her nails into the sheets, and shadows dip the room into silence. I kiss her thigh before pushing her legs down so she can't move. "Come for me, witch."

I slide two fingers into her just as I suck on her clit, and she screams my name. "Lysander!" Male satisfaction spreads through me as she comes on my face, on my fingers, and fuck does she feel tight. I can't wait. I need to feel her around my cock. I stand up, pushing down my trousers. My witch is quick, leaning forward and wrapping her lips around the tip of my cock, all the while looking up at me with a taunting gaze. I grip her hair and force her to slide her lips down, my cock slipping deeper into her hot mouth, and I drop my head back as my balls feel ready to burst. One suck, one fucking slip into my mate's mouth, and I'm fucking ready to come.

The witch damn well knows it, increasing her speed and driving me crazy. I lift her up off the bed, parting her legs and slamming my cock inside her as my hand finds her neck. She moans as she takes me, and I fuck her like a man possessed. She moans and tightens around me already, and I want this to last. I know it won't, as my balls argue with all logic. She moans louder as I rub my thumb across her clit, thrusting my cock in and out of her. She cries out my name as she comes and tightens around my cock, making it impossible to do anything but let myself come. I roar as I come, intense pleasure slamming down my spine, and I nearly fucking pass out with how good she feels. I'm obsessed and I don't care if she knows it.

Fucking my mate is like an out-of-body experience, and I won't ever tire of this. We collapse together on the bed, and she wraps her legs around my waist, tempting me for round two. I'll convince her in a minute. "I love you but tell me everything."

I bury my face in her hair, enjoying her scent. Especially now she smells like my seed, too. "I won. I don't mean the test, but I did also win that. You're mine."

She doesn't disagree.

CHAPTER 6

LIVIA

"*Y*ou look serious and it's ruining our romantic meeting place."

Jinks makes me jump, and I know the sneaky bastard came up here as a cat so I wouldn't hear them and then shifted back. They are in their female form now, all long white curly hair and pretty eyes. I'm not sure which gender I like the most, but I know I'm deeply attached to everything Jinks.

Jinks has a way of appearing any time that I'm upset, or just appearing in general when I leave my room. They bump my shoulder as they stop at my side, looking over the Spirit Court. It's dark out, the sun long past set. "I didn't tell you about Florence yet, and I want to. She was beautiful and brave, and I liked her from the moment she told me she didn't want to be a queen and she wasn't marrying any man."

They softly smile at me. "Sounds like a woman who knew her mind. I take it she is in the afterlife now?"

I nod. "She died in the earth test, while I was thrown to the West to be protected by the castle. I don't blame the castle, but I wish it took her too." I look at the stone under my hands. "Arty killed her, and sometimes when I see her, I want to get revenge."

"Say the word and I'll do it for you," they offer. They aren't joking, and it makes me smile that they would murder for me.

I shake my head at them. "It's complicated and I know Arty…well, I think Florence would tell me to forgive her. It's just hard."

"Forgiveness is an easy word but an uneasy emotion to accept," Jinks adds, covering my hand with theirs. We stare at each other for a long moment, and my eyes drop to their lips, which are painted red and remind me of exactly what Jinks is. A demon. Maybe it's normal to be this insanely attracted to an ancient seduction demon who looks at me like they want to eat me literally all of the time. I find myself searching for them in every room, at every meal, and I barely stay in my room anymore because there is more chance of finding Jinks outside it. "Are you concerned about tomorrow?"

"I am. It's good that Lysander passed the first test, but tomorrow's fire, and Elle's going with him. That can't be a good thing."

Jinks looks away at the sky. "King Arden won't let anything happen to his mate, but I know how much you care about her and this court. I don't know if a demon praying is worth anything, but I will pray for your queen to win this all with her kings."

"Did I ever tell you that I became slightly obsessed with how incredible she is?" I mutter. "Jealous, maybe."

"You've got no reason to be jealous. You are incredible," Jinks firmly finishes. "Livia, I—"

"Ah...there you both are," Elle's grandmother interrupts without a care in the world that I desperately want to know what Jinks was going to say. Hera is wearing only a white dressing gown, with a sunflower snap claw holding her hair up in a mess. I don't even want to know what she just finished with her creepy god mate she brought here. "I need a bit of your blood, Jinks and Livia. Let in the god I'm about to summon."

"Why?" Jinks questions, cocking their head to the side. I almost forgot that these two have lived together for a long time. She kind of treats them like a wayward teenager she had custody of for a time. It's cute.

"We need Phobos here. It turns out a bit of blood from hell's creatures and Cronus's special touch can make a potion to summon any god to this world through the barriers. These are the rest of the ingredients." She shakes a vial of red liquid. "Chop chop, kitty cat. I have a mate to return to and plans to set in motion."

Gross.

I clear my throat. "Does Elle know he is coming?"

"No, it's a surprise. Don't ruin it." Hera waves me off. "And for heaven's sake, stop worrying in that mind of yours. Yes, he is the god of horror, but he can behave. He has a new mate now, who's human. So he knows what it's like to have someone to lose, plus he's very fond of Elle, and she is his niece. He's brought her up with me, and we need all the family here now for what's coming."

Jinks doesn't hesitate before offering her their hand, and Hera cuts their fingertip quickly with a sharp spike of one of the many rings on her hand, before plopping a drop of their blood in the vial, which glows a burning red before she smashes it on the ground. The vial sends red smoke soaring until a portal appears, and a flutter in my chest warns me someone is coming through the barrier. It's easy to stop him if I wanted, just to connect to the magic and will it to snap shut.

When the ward fell, so did I. It felt like someone tore a hole in my chest and I couldn't breathe. It was a spell, and it didn't last long once Aphrodite left. I put the ward right back up and thanked the good gods in the sky for being lucky enough not to die.

The smoky portal clears with the wind, and on the other side is a stunning, dangerous-looking man sitting on a pumpkin in a forest. Dark hair, long legs, and all in black, with something terrifying in his dark eyes that makes me shiver. Jinks moves closer and I'm thankful for them.

At his side is a young woman who looks like she lives in a Halloween shop. She has a checkered skirt that stops at her thighs, fishnet tights, a dark black crop top that matches the colour of her dark hair, all curled up at her back of the neck. His hand is possessively around her waist as he looks through and sighs, rising to whisper in her ear. They kiss passionately for a minute, and I look away. When I look back, he's walking through the portal alone. It snaps shut behind him. "I gather there's a way I go back soon?"

The world feels darker, more sinister, the second he is here.

"Go back whenever you want, after you've killed people for your niece." Hera grins and it makes her look young. "Darling, it is always a pleasure to see you. Thank you for coming."

He crosses his bulky arms. "I trained Ellelin to kill a fuck ton of people on her own. Why can't she do that and I go back to my mate?"

"Phobos."

"Mother."

They glare at each other before she hugs him, and he clearly gives in, even when he doesn't hug her back. Hera pats his arm before she steps away. Phobos drags his eyes to Jinks. "Are you behaving, cat?"

They bow their head. "Always."

The god of nightmares looks at me, and I feel like my blood freezes in fear. I can barely move under his gaze. "Is this the mate you came through for?"

The shock of that statement makes me force myself to look at Jinks with a will power that apparently can defy the gods. What the fuck? "Mate?"

CHAPTER 7

The dream appears like any other, except for everything's different. It feels like Emrys, like he's right there in front of me and all around me at the same time. It's because he is. We're standing on a boat, a creaky, wide, wooden boat, in what looks like a foggy lake. The fog's slowly moving around like small waves, but the boat doesn't move. Emrys is on the other side of the boat, just standing there, and he looks so real it breaks me. He's wearing a white shirt tucked into tight black trousers. His hands are resting in his pockets, and when he smiles at me, warmness flows through my body. I smile back at him. I want this not to be a dream, but to be real. When I wake up, Emrys is still going to be trapped in his body with Ares ruling.

"It's really me. You need to go into the darkness and I'll be there." He walks across the boat. The darkness? How could he be down there? The boat doesn't move; it doesn't tip or rock in the water like a normal boat would do when someone moves. There's nothing around us, just more fog. Endless, endless fog. Why this place? His hands sink into my hair, and his touch feels right. Just so right. He pulls me to him; his lips are on mine within a second, a mixture of a soft pressure but a little more than that and everything Emrys. Just everything. I moan as he pushes us down, only to turn us so he is sitting on the bench and I spread my legs around him, my white dress pooling at my thighs. I never wear dresses like this. "How are you here? Is this real?"

"I'm always real to you," he promises, running his teeth across my bottom lip. "We don't have much time," he whispers, kissing down my neck. "I just, I need you to remember this. Remember me here. It's not just a dream and you need to remember."

He keeps kissing me like it's our last kiss,

like he needs every moment, and I breathe in his scent, how he smells so normal. I miss him so much. How is this possible? "What are you talking about?"

Emrys's hands drift slowly down my body before pushing up the white dress that I'm wearing. His hand slides my underwear to the side, and I gasp as he slips his finger into my folds, finding my clit and stroking it as I moan. "You need to remember this, and I won't let you forget." The pleasure is intense, and I moan again, which he captures with his mouth. He rips the underwear off, undoing his trousers and pulling me to him. I slowly sink onto his cock, inch by inch, my cheeks flushing. He grabs my ass, pulling me up and down on him, and I'm so close. "You need to remember." He groans against my lips. "Fuck, don't forget me. This."

"Never," I cry out as I orgasm and he crashes with me, just as the dream fades.

I wake up panting as I stare up at the ceiling and look around. "Emrys?"

Nothing answers me, and I sink my head back on the pillow. Of course he isn't here. My door is knocked twice, and I groan, sliding out of the bed with the dream replaying over and over in my mind. It was him; I know it, but how? He is trapped in his body with Ares in control. So how did he pull me into a dream like that? It felt like more than a dream though, like a memory instead, but one I've never lived. I should have told him I loved him. I should have told him over and over that I loved him. Why didn't I say that?

How could he ever think I'd forget him? Never. Ever. Gods, Emrys.

"Just a moment," I tell whoever was knocking. I quickly run to the bathroom and get changed for the day before opening the door and finding my uncle outside. "Phobos?" I blurt out. "What are you doing here?"

"Surprise. Your castle is fucking nosy and gave me a towel this morning before I even got out of the shower. Do you think it watches?" The castle corridor goes cold and the floorboards creak under his feet as I shake my head at him before hugging him. He doesn't hug me back. He never does. He's not a hugger. But I think he appreciates the sentiment anyway. "I'm here to help you win a war and kill people. The second part I find fun—and my mate usually tells me no."

"Where is your mate?" I ask. I'm glad he is here, and we definitely could do with the god of nightmares on our side in a war. "Is she in the castle somewhere?" I ask as we begin heading down the corridor.

"No." He frowns. "I love her. I'm not bringing her to a world at war. Would you really bring any of your mates here if you had any other choice?"

"Touché." I sigh, resting my head on his shoulder. "Where is my grandmother, anyway?"

"Disgustingly in love with an old god," he replies. "It sickens me."

My shoulders drop a little when I see my mates, and the tension drifts away as we get to the dining room. Phobos doesn't come in with me, choosing to stay outside instead. Grayson is sitting at the dinner table with toast and bacon on his plate, Lysander is sipping on a coffee, and there is another coffee laid out in the empty seat between, along with a plate full of my favourite breakfast choices. Arden is sitting on the other side, leaning back in his seat, and he looks over his shoulder when I come in. "I didn't want to wake you. She can wait."

"I'd rather not eat and just get going now," I

admit, but Grayson pulls out the seat next to him and challenges me with one look to try to walk out without eating something. I sigh and sit down, sipping on the perfect temperature coffee until it wakes me up. "I think Emrys spoke to me in my dreams last night. I don't understand how it happened, but it did. He warned me that I need to go into the darkness below and he will be there. His soul will."

Lysander and Arden share a look. "We just spoke about how you scented like Emrys in your sleep. It was strange."

"He is still fighting, and he won't stop." It brings me a new feeling of strength, knowing I wasn't just imagining him there, kissing me, telling me he will never give up on us. On a future for us. Reluctantly, I eat some of the food, which tastes like ash in my mouth with how nervous I am. "I'm done. Can we go now?"

Arden nods, rising to his feet. He looks like a handsome dude ready to go to a party, not a battle. He has not bothered to wear his leather protective clothing or any armour. Instead, he has a nice crisp red silk shirt on, tucked into tight black trousers that fit his muscular body perfectly. I, on the other hand, decided fire proof leathers from my neck to my boots were a better plan. The black fabric sticks to me and makes me feel like I'm boiling underneath it, but I prefer that over being burnt. I tug at the collar as I stand up, brushing my other hand over Grayson's shoulder to say goodbye. We both know he doesn't do goodbyes, and I hate them, too. Lysander wraps his hand around my hip, turning me towards him. "If it helps, you look absolutely sensational in that."

"It really does not," I mutter, but I can't help but smile. "What are your plans for the day?"

"Fixing my court," Lysander offers. I wince, wondering how he plans to fix anything there. "And paying a visit to my mother with letters from Kian, as he plans to stay here with Artemis until their wedding."

I'm still getting used to the idea Arty is going to be my sister-in-law. Everything is messy between us, and I don't know how I could ever fully trust her again. I know that's what she wants, and I have forgiven her as best I can for what she did...but she took lives. She also saved lives. She saved Emrys at the risk of her own life. Sometimes I look at her and still see my friend who betrayed me, and other times,

I see a sister. When she becomes my sister-in-law, that will be forever. I know time will heal. I just hope we have that time. I lean down and kiss him softly. "Don't kill them all."

"No promises, spirit witch," he grumbles like I've just ruined his fun.

Arden takes my hand, and I only look once over my shoulder at my mates before going right through a portal to the Air Court with Arden. We both brace ourselves because of what happened to Lysander, but we step out into the throne room, and it's empty. Silent. I can smell death in the air, and the court that used to sing with life is silent like a grave. "We're going to be fine," Arden reassures me.

"You have far more confidence in this than I do," I whisper, turning my gaze up to Arden's. The wind howls around us, blowing my braid across my back, and his eyes waver. The confidence that's coming out of his mouth doesn't match the feeling I get. He is scared for me. We both know this is terrifying, but we have survived so, so much. We will survive this. At least he's putting a brave face on, whereas I am not exactly doing that, and I need to. Aphrodite is like a dog searching for a bone when it comes to her enemies' weaknesses. I lift my head and look forward.

"Do you think if we just went downstairs, rescued your mother and Gray's sister, she'd notice?" Arden half jokes. "I'm good with locks, princess."

I grin at him. "If she leaves us here any longer, I might be tempted to try."

Arden links our hands, our fingers woven and locked tight. Whatever the test is, we will deal with it together one final time. If it's a fire element test, like Lysander battled with his element, then we'll be in the best of company.

Aphrodite appears like she's gliding through the air, like she's taken over the element itself as well as the court. It makes me grit my teeth, especially because Emrys is holding her hand as they walk down together. He looks pale, sickly almost, in dark clothes that don't suit him. His cheeks are hollowed in like he's not been eating, and his skin is borderline grey. The sight of him makes me literally feel sick to my stomach. It's been days, just days, and he already looks like this. What the hell are they doing to him?

"Is my friend's body not sitting comfortably with you?" Arden growls before Aphrodite can say a word. "You probably should know taking over a king who desperately wants to get back to his mate was a stupid fucking idea. You look like you're close to death, god of war. Weak."

Ares stumbles forward, and his wife has to hold him up for a second. I stare at Emrys like he was really in front of me. I speak right to him. "We're going to save you. Keep fighting."

"Shut up, the pair of you," Aphrodite snaps at me, her cheeks burning red. A pissed goddess is a dangerous one and also one who makes mistakes. "All souls fade in the end."

I shake my head at her, knowing that Emrys won't. I tell myself to remember the dream I had this morning, which felt so real. It was real, at least that's what I'm going to tell myself. I didn't imagine it. Emrys was there in my mind, somehow fighting through, telling me he's never going to give up on me. Like I'd never give up on him. I believe we are destined for a long life together.

She waves her hand, and an archway appears right on the edge of the rock. The archway, made of shining red rocks, glitters in the sunlight. On the other side is a pit of darkness, and I can't see through it. "I'm bored with conversations when you are pushing on my nerves. Go through and face your test."

Arden looks at the goddess one more time. "You will burn in dragon fire for eternity for touching our world." There is power in the words of a fire king, making a threat on the very element that bows to him. The world warms for a second and Aphrodite blanches, taking a step back. The king of fire looks down at me, and I feel captivated by his stare. "Whatever happens in there, don't leave my side. We fight as one."

"My fire mate," I whisper. Our fingers link together tightly as we step through the arch and into the darkness. It's warm, ridiculously warm. I frown as I see it's a room that looks like a classroom, with desks and rows of bookcases, science-like ornaments everywhere. There is a thick layer of dust and cobwebs on everything here, and I just know no one has been here in a long time. All I can smell is fire though, and smoke. So much smoke. "This reminds me of the first test I took for the crown." I walk over to the nearest window, looking down. Except outside, it isn't the spirit castle. It's just pits of lava inside a massive volcano.

Arden's pale when I look at him. He turns

from me, slamming his fists on the stone wall where the arch just was. "You bitch. You fucking bitch."

I run over, touching his shoulder and sliding between him and the wall so he has to look at me. "Arden...what is this place?"

His voice is hoarse. "The home of my only surviving family. My great-grandfather. His name was Marcelli." I don't understand why that's a problem, why Arden looks spooked. "My father showed me this place once before, along with the family secret, because he thought every ruling royal needed to see what happens when you stretch your magic too far. When you become the fire and touch a deeper part of our fire magic than is advised." I still don't understand. "This place is a volcano, deep in the north part of my realm where some people from my court live, but it's mostly deserted. It's a grave."

"Why? What happened?"

"It was a school for teenagers to learn with the king, to experiment with our fire element in uncontrolled manners. The strongest of my court was sent here. It was meant to be a place of hope." He looks down. "Underneath it is a monster and death. They all died except for him."

I don't want to look at the creaky floorboards. "What kind of monster?"

"Marcelli. He is transformed into his dragon form by the death and magic, a spell so strong no one could break it and survive. He is one with the flame at the very core of this court. He couldn't shift back due to the magic of this place, and he eats or burns anybody that comes here except for me and the descendants of the teenagers who died here." He grits his teeth. "Aphrodite wanted you to come today because she knew you are neither of those things. My great-grandfather is going to attack you, and I'll have to kill the only blood family I have left alive. If 'alive' even means anything to him at this point."

"We probably have not long before he's going to come up here and start attacking us?" I question.

"If I shift, I won't be able to shift back within the volcano, and the magic might latch onto me and force me to stay in my dragon form. I—" Arden pauses. "My father was warned by his father never to shift here. I never asked more and didn't have time to before he was dead."

"Lucky your mate can make a shadow dragon, then, huh?" I question. "We can just fly the fuck away from here." I know it won't be that simple, but still, it's worth a shot. "We can ride it together. I've never done it, but I think it will be fine. Just pushing my limits, and that's a good thing."

"Will your dragon be able to attack a fully grown male dragon as big as what my great-granddad's dragon will be like?" Arden right-fully asks, his eyes wide. "I won't risk you. Anyone touches you and they die, that means family too. You're my entire world, the beginning and end. I'll shift first and risk it all to save you."

My heart leaps. Family is everything to Arden, especially because he has none left. I understand why he doesn't count his great-grandfather as being alive when he is in this state and the fact he would kill him to save me... I take his hand and lean into his body. "I love you and it won't come to that."

I'll make sure of it.

Arden cups my cheek and I melt for him, almost forgetting the seriousness of the situation we are in. "I don't know how much is left of his mind, but it won't be a lot. All I know is he's ancient, stubborn, and was even before his final shift, from what my father told me. He is all dragon and a hunter. We—" The floor underneath us starts to shake, and Arden cuts himself off. The books, clutter on the desks, and glass vials lining the sides slam onto the floor one by one. "Princess, don't you dare leave my side."

The walls themselves start cracking, but I look away from the danger and to my fire mate for a second. "Don't shift."

He smirks at me, even with pain shining in his eyes. "If there is a choice between saving your life and becoming a dragon here trapped forever...I'm shifting."

"Arden"—I shake my head before I lean up on my tiptoes, and I kiss him, just softly brushing my lips on his—"we leave here together, or not at all."

"Princess, I love you too. I have done since you got mad at me for burning your ex." He steps back. "Still don't regret that. I would have killed him anyway for touching you."

Shaking my head, I put the memories of that day behind me, even knowing he is telling me the truth. If Arden hadn't killed him, I would put money on Lysander or Grayson doing it. Emrys, he might have just made him disappear. "You're possessive."

"Proudly." Arden grins. "Show me what a good spirit princess you are. Call the shadows."

I grin at him, knowing that we're in this together and nothing can stop us. It doesn't take long for me to pull shadows, like they have been waiting for me, begging me to embrace them. I pull them and whisper around me, spreading them out across the room until giant wings are pushing against the boundaries of the brick, cracking them. Arden comes with me to climb onto the back, which feels solid, yet it's nothing but spinning shadows constantly moving to make a dragon body. Its shadow tail tears through the back wall of the room, sending bricks and roof flying everywhere. It roars like it's alive, like it's not just my magic and it's a real being I've pulled from the shadows.

Thank any gods that still listen for my shadows, because the floor suddenly gives in. Nothing but balls of flames shoot out of the floorboards until the room is red with flames, and smoke is hovering around us like a fog. A scream echoes out of my throat. I can't help it and Arden grips me tightly down onto the dragon from behind, right as my dragon jumps up and uses shadows to propel us up in the air, crashing through the roof. Bricks, sharp rock, and who knows what else fall on my body as we burst out of the top of the room. Lava shoots high up into the air, narrowly missing us as my dragon swerves to the right and rises higher, giving me a good look at the tower we just escaped from. It reminds me of Rapunzel's tower, but the top is now caved in and it's sinking into the lava. Arden holds his hand out, and the pools of lava instantly drop away under his command.

We turn around and come face to face with a dragon that is nearly the image of Arden's, but it's a giant in comparison. This monster dragon, with chipped, burnt black scales and a red line of spikes down its back, was once a Fire Court king. Now there's nothing much left to him except his dragon form. His eyes are glazed darkness, not red like Arden's. Arden once told me all the kings in his family have those red eyes, and this must be what happened to him under the spell. He lost himself to the fire, and his eyes are proof. He is terrifying, sending a cold chill down my spine. Instinctively, shadows rise in every direction of the volcano, swirling up in the air to meet my call. I take a deep breath of the smoky air as Arden links his hand through mine on my dragon. "I'm going to need a bigger dragon."

I feel the tingling of the power down my spine as I pull the rising shadows to me, to my dragon, and it grows under us, spreading out its now massive wings. More and more shadows come to my dragon. It's almost mimicking the size of Marcelli, but I make sure to wrap darkness around us, protecting Arden. Protecting my mate.

Marcelli roars at us, spitting fire before diving straight off the cliff edge of the volcano and straight our way. My dragon spirals to the side, its claws ripping across Marcelli's giant wing. Marcelli roars louder, shaking the volcano around us, creating massive cracks right in the edges, just before he crashes into the side of the volcano, rock spitting into the lava that pools around him. The lava and fire don't hurt this dragon; he simply shakes it off with a growl. Arden isn't watching Marcelli though, his eyes are down. "There's a fucking village down there!"

I look down, my heart racing, and I see he's right, there's a village at the bottom of the volcano just below where Marcelli has crashed. His big body is holding the fire back, but the moment he flies, that lava is going to pour down to destroy the village. Without saying a word to Arden, knowing he will agree, I turn my shadow dragon straight towards the village to warn them. The force of swooping down on a dragon this big feels like the pressure and wind is ripping apart my skin, and I grit my teeth all the way down. When we are close to the village, Arden's shout finally reaches my ears. "I can hold the lava back for at least ten minutes!"

"I'll distract Marcelli and get him as far away from the volcano as I can. I'll give you all the time you can get, but Arden, who knows how she spelled this place? She could have added to your grandfather's spell. She could have made it so that if you shift anywhere near here, you get trapped in your dragon form. I don't want that, so do not shift and come after me."

The wind roars around us as Arden leans in and kisses me softly before jumping right off the side of my dragon before I can even grab him. Arden flies down, landing smoothly on a tiled roof and rising to his feet. His hands glow like red burning stars, and he faces them towards the volcano. The red light spreads down his body, making every inch of him glow until he looks like a fire god. The lava actually stops in its tracks, a wall of fire spreading around the volcano, and it's impressive.

As much as it scares me how much power Arden is using, I shouldn't have taken my eyes off Marcelli, because the big old bastard is right on my heels when I glance back, and I push my dragon to fly away as fast as possible. We dive over the town, leaving a wave of glittering darkness in our wake. I spin back to the volcano, narrowly missing Marcelli's claw and the blast of fire he sends in my direction. When I spin around, my eyes widen at Marcelli, who has somehow turned faster than I did, and he is about to crash right into me.

Into the village right behind me and Arden.

Desperately, I pull all my shadows to make a wall, but he's too fast, cutting through them with fire, and I'm about to scream when a familiar beautiful black dragon dives into his side, sending them both rolling in the opposite direction. "ARDEN!"

My scream is lost to the wind, and I'm stuck, unable to do anything but watch as the dragons fight with fire, claws and teeth. I focus on the village, knowing I can't let those innocents die and Arden needs me to save them. The lava is slower than I'd expect it to be, but it's still coming down the volcano, and they won't get far enough on foot.

There's people already screaming, running out of the houses as I land on a fountain, crushing it with my shadow dragon. Sweat pours down my face, and I feel breathless from using so much power, but I start making a box of shadows big enough for at least a hundred people and add something for my dragon to hold on to at the top. Everything is spinning around me when I'm done, but I see the crowd. I see the scared children, the cowering adults, and a sea of redheads who don't know where to turn. "Everyone get on the dragon. I'm Ellelin, Princess of the Spirit Court and King Arden's mate. Trust me or trust him. Just get in and I'll save you."

I'm surprised when they actually run towards my terrible box. That looks like hell itself. Even the children fight their parents in fear, but they don't run away. Only when it's silent and no one else comes closer, only when the sound of lava cracking stone gets closer, do I force my dragon up into the air, feeling like I'm touching the edges of my magic, like it's all too much. I need more power for this. My shoulders drop, and my dragon groans as I nearly fall forward. I shake my head and grit my teeth, pushing the last dregs of my power into getting my shadow dragon to pick up the box and fly it high into the sky.

People scream and cry, but I block out the terrible sound of their fear and keep my dragon going. I keep going, keep pushing, tasting blood in my mouth. Feeling blood pouring from my nose and ears. When I see water, with a dock and two ships, I finally let my dragon slowly drop the box and let the magic go, shadows disappearing around all the people I've saved. I slump on my dragon as they cheer, as they shout for me and Arden, but I don't hear anything other than my desperate need to see my mate.

"Arden..." I turn my shadow dragon back, straight towards Arden. I can see Arden's dragon and his grandfather's fighting, the two of them lashing out against each other, but pride fills me as I realise Arden is fast, quick, and he's a king. Fire bends to him, swirling round in great arcs around the dragons, smothering Marcelli as it pushes him down to the floor. Arden's gorgeous dragon lets out a mighty roar as he lands on top of Marcelli, pushing him down on the ground, lava pooling. He watches me until I'm close, and I land on his back, finally letting my shadow dragon disappear and the power too. I wipe my blood away as I look at Marcelli and feel his chest moving up and down. This grandfather dragon is so big. One of his teeth is probably the size of me, and he isn't dead.

"Shift back!" I shout at Arden. The dragon shakes his head. My heart races at the stubborn red glowing eyes. "Shift back!"

He does. I've never been so happy to see the mist around his dragon and, when it fades, to see Arden. My smile fades when Aphrodite steps out of a portal next to Arden, who comes straight to my side and wraps his arm around my waist, holding me up. I need him too, I realise. I've pushed my magic too far. Aphrodite looks down, disgust marking her pretty face until it makes her look as ugly as her heart is. "Kill him and you win. Both of you never thought to ask what the actual terms of the test were."

Arden feels like he goes cold at my side. "I'm not killing my grandfather."

She smiles. "So, you lose? Honestly, there is nothing left of him in here, anyway. Kill him or you lose."

I close my eyes. We only have to win three out of the four, and we just lost this one. "He's not killing him, and neither am I. You win, you fucking bitch."

"Elle," Arden whispers to me.

I look into Arden's red eyes. "He's your grandfather. You should have told me about him before now, and we'll figure out a way to break the spell, because you need family. We can lose one." His eyes are filled with love and pride.

Aphrodite is smug, and it grates on my last nerves. "Fine, go back then."

A portal opens right under our feet. I scream as I fall straight through the air. Not with Arden, just on my own. I'm right above the spirit castle, far above it, and my magic is weak. "Terrin!" I scream in my mind for him. "Terrin, I can't call my shadows."

I try to pull my shadows, try several times, but they just crash underneath me with how weak they are. I scream as I keep falling. Just as the castle comes into view, Terrin sweeps out of the clouds, catching me mid-air. I knock my chin on his face, tasting more blood in my mouth, and my teeth sting from the impact. My entire body hurts, in fact. I groan as I hold on to him.

"What the fuck are you doing up in the sky? Are you okay?"

"Yes, just fancied learning to fly," I joke, and he growls loudly. I sigh, resting my head on his back. "Aphrodite opened a portal unexpectedly. We lost the test."

"I'm sorry," Terrin answers. "And fucking hell, when can we kill her?"

"Soon," I vow.

"I think it's about time I tell you every-thing," Terrin softly whispers into my mind as I spot Arden's dragon flying with Grayson around the castle, both of them heading our way. "And please don't hate me."

CHAPTER 8

HOPE

"Why are we locked in a room?" I lean back on the wall, by the window. "Again?"

Xandry is sitting on the edge of the bed, a sea blue sword resting across his knees, and he is quietly wiping the blood off the blade as he lifts his eyes to meet mine, and like usual, I can't look away even if I wanted to. He has a way of pulling me in, and he always has done, but at least I have the answer to why. He is my mate. He is the one I'm destined to be with, and this obsession I have is normal. Dreaming about him? Normal. Wanting to jump him even when we aren't alone? Borderline insane. "Because we were nearly killed only an hour ago, and murdering more of them is a shit idea. We stay in here and call for help from the Spirit Court and our friends."

"Assassinations seem to be a problem," Meredith mutters, like she wasn't the one they nearly killed. If I hadn't heard her scream, I doubt Xandry and I would have been able to save her in time. There were twelve of them, and Xandry took out nine. The smug bastard hasn't mentioned the difference, but I know he will. We've been back only a few days, and the fucking nobles have made it very clear we aren't welcome. First, it was blocking us from having any food by claiming there was none and locking the kitchens for anyone but them. Then, it was flooding several royal quarters where they assumed we would be sleeping, but we weren't, thank the dragon gods. Today, they just sent assassins to deal with us. "The nobles have gotten used to ruling on their own. They, of course, didn't take it too well when I told them all he's back in this world and a little angry."

"Well, would you have taken it well when you're practically ruling?" Xandry questions. "They are stupid assholes. Sorry about my language, your majesty, but they are. Nothing will ever change, and you telling them that news without King Lysander here was risky."

"My son needs a council, and he set all of us up with this task." She lifts her head high. "And —" She pauses and looks behind her at the door that leads to the main corridor of the castle. Cold salt water pours through the gap beneath the door. I frown, looking down at the clear water, and notice right away how it doesn't touch us. It skirts around our feet, leaving a dry path on the floor at our feet. "The water king is back."

She looks proud, even when we all hear it. The screaming. The screaming doesn't last long, and I wince. Lysander isn't known for being merciful. Meredith opens the door, and we all see a waterfall going down the middle of the corridor, taking people with it. The water unnaturally glows with magic, and I'm familiar enough with Lysander's magic to know it is his.

Xandry moves close to my side, and we watch as Meredith steps out the door and the water parts around her as she walks. I rush with Xandry to stay close behind her, following her all the way down to the flooded throne room where Lysander's lounging in his chair, his chin resting on his fist. Hundreds of nobles are in puddles of water at the bottom of the court. All of the water council, all the men and women who have been ruling this place when they had no right to. They might be born nobles, but they never worked a day in their lives, never fought or defended anyone but themselves. I don't think there is a friendly soul among them anymore, and if there was, they would have disappeared by now for not being like them.

"Your highness." One of them stands.

Xandry leans into me. "Noble Christopher Icedriften."

I like how he knows I wouldn't have a clue what this one's name is. I gather he is their leader. He doesn't bow and I cross my arms at the insult to our king. Christopher is a chubby man with a rounded stomach, and all of him is stuffed into a dark blue suit. He runs a hand through his grey hair, what is left of it, and smiles at Lysander like a snake who isn't bothering to hide their teeth. Does he really think he could take on Lysander and win? Fool. "What are you doing here?"

Lysander laughs, and the sound echoes. It isn't a humoured laugh, but one of shock and surprise with a hint of darkness. "What am I doing here, in my own fucking court?" Lysander leans forward and puts his hands on the sides of the throne. Fury makes him look every bit like an angry king. "Let me think. Oh wait, what was the plan again? Yes, I remember now. I'm getting rid of all of you. I'm stripping my court from the generations of evil that have dampened this place and made it a cursed pit of bullshit betrayers who deserve nothing."

"You can't do that!" he splutters, and they all start panicking. A few reach for their powers to attack Lysander, but they don't work. This is Lysander's court, and the water only bows to him in here. Idiots, the lot of them.

"I absolutely fucking can. I own everything here. If I want to drown this entire island, which I'm fucking tempted to, I will." He leans back. "But my mate would be pissed if I did that, and I promised her I wouldn't murder everyone. Aren't you fucking lucky she is so merciful?"

It's really hard not to laugh. I can imagine Elle told him to behave, and clearly, he loves her enough to do so. "So, you're all banished from Ayiolyn. Refuse, and you're dead. I don't really give a shit either way."

"Banished?" Christopher shouts. "You can't do that to us! We are your court, your nobles!"

"You are my father's court, and you each are the bastards he chose because of how fucked up each of you are. That ends today and so does his hold on me and this court." I'm oddly proud of Lysander right now. I cast a glance at his mum, and she has tears in her eyes, along with a bright smile. She looks happier than I've ever seen her. Meredith has always struggled with her mental health since her king died, and I wonder how deep the evil in this place runs and how far it has pushed her down.

"Your father was the greatest—"

"My father was a shit king, and I will not be him." Lysander cuts him off. "I made a deal with a certain god of nightmares and..." He clicks his fingers, and a portal appears to the side of the throne. "You step through this portal with no powers and fuck all anything. You will go and live out the rest of your pathetic lives in one of the shittiest places on Earth. You will be human and die of old age with no magic to keep you alive longer. There is no magic on Earth left." I look through the barrier, seeing a small town on the other side. It doesn't exactly look pleasant. There's rubbish rolling down the streets in the wind. "Go."

Christopher runs up the steps, nearly slipping in the water. He throws himself on his knees, bowing his head. "Please, please stop this and forgive us. What about our children?"

"Your children belong to the Water Court, and they can stay here. They're not complete dickheads yet, and I will find them therapists to deal with the memories of you lot. They can stay in the court and take over your places if they earn it." Lysander cocks his head to the side. "Now get the fuck out of my court."

"You can't do this!" Christopher screams, pulling out a dagger and heading for Lysander.

Lysander yawns and wraps magic around Christopher, holding him in the air. "Yes, I absolutely can. I'm sure you're not that worried about your kids. Most of them are in the boarding schools littered around the courts, and I know for a fact you don't see them, anyway. Too busy, I assume."

"I will never stop until I kill you and your queen!" Christopher yells, and it's his last words. Threatening Elle? A really stupid move. Christopher starts spurting water out of his mouth, coughing and choking on it right before he goes still. Lysander drops him on the throne steps and looks around the nobles. "Who's next then?"

They all get up and run to the portal like their asses are on fire. I actually think this is the most merciful I've ever seen Lysander. Has everything to do with Elle. Usually, he wouldn't have hesitated before just killing them all. But here he is. Rather than killing them, he's giving them a chance at a new life, even if the bastards don't want it. It takes a while for the hundreds of nobles in here to flood through the portal to Earth before Lysander closes it. The body of Christopher floats in the water and down a river straight to the sea.

"Did you mean it?" Meredith asks, walking to her son.

He stands up and faces her. "Why didn't you tell me about your firstborn? Why didn't you grieve with me?"

Xandry and I glance at each other. I want to walk out and leave them to it, but they haven't asked us to leave yet. Meredith sobs and Lysander pulls her into his arms, holding her as she cries for a long time. "I never grieved. Your father, he used magic to make me forget your sister, and when he died, the memories came back. I didn't want to make you hate him, and I didn't know how to tell you that I failed to protect your sister. I remember her now, and she looked like Kian. She was bright and smart... and she's gone. I'm sorry."

Lysander rests his chin on her head, his own cheeks wet with quiet tears. "No more lies, no more secrets, and our family is going to move on from him. He is dead, and it's about time we worked on a future. I want you to be at my mating party with Elle, and I want you at every special occasion. I want you here, ruling in my absence and making the decisions. I want my mother."

"I'm here," she whispers. "And I'm never letting you down again." Xandry leans over and wipes my cheek of the tear I didn't even know I had cried, and I lean my head on his arm, watching as so many cracks in the heart of the Water Court are fixed. "I appreciate you coming in and getting rid of all our problems. But now we have additional problems. Who's going to rule in your stead while you're at a Spirit Court with no nobles here? I can, but not alone."

Lysander straightens and points at us. "Hope and Xandry. You're now new nobles. Choose whatever land and houses you want to have. I don't care. They are the head of the council, and they can go around these lands and pick whoever the fuck you want to be a noble as long as they aren't assholes. I trust you both along with my mother's guidance." I feel like he means more than just giving us those titles. His eyes flicker to my head on Xandry's arm, and he smiles at me. I smile back. "I'm going to the kitchens because the Spirit Court castle really can't make the chocolate cake that my mate liked, and I'm going to take it back to her after she finishes the fire test."

"Tell her…" I pause. "Well, she knows, but good luck."

Lysander nods. "I will." He walks out with his mother, and I watch until they have left.

"Do you still love him?" Xandry's question catches me off guard. I turn around, the water puddling at my feet now.

Xandry waits patiently for my answer. I frown at him. He thinks I love Lysander. "No." I say the word firmly. "We were a distraction to each other, and I was using him to make me feel like I had a home and wasn't alone. I wanted so desperately to hold on to the family I found here that I couldn't see I was poisoning it. I need to tell you something." I clear my throat and just go for it. "I don't love Lysander, not like that, not anymore." I look at this man who literally followed me across worlds and asked for nothing even when we are mates. "I liked you back then. When we were teenagers. In fact, I was a little obsessed with you, and you were my best friend for a reason. Lysander was easier than admitting that I liked you, because I thought if I told you and you rejected me, then I'd lose everything I wanted. There'd be nothing left. So, I went for the easier option, even though I didn't really feel that much. I forced myself to because I wanted you. I was so angry when I saw you again in the spirit castle as our tutor because you dared to live without me. You didn't look for me, you gave up!" He goes still. "What I'm trying to say is that I love you. I've been falling for you for what feels like forever, and being vulnerable with my feelings is not something I do well, or even know how to do."

He steps into my space and grasps my upper arms. His eyes seem to stare into my soul. "I loved you back then and I love you now. I want a future with you here, in this court where we both grew up and it became our home. You are my mate and if you'll accept me, I'll never stop loving and protecting you, Hope. I want everything."

Xandry kisses me, and it feels like coming home. It feels like the moment I've waited for, the person I've been looking for, and from today, I'm no longer searching for my home. It's him.

CHAPTER 9

J use my magic to transform Terrin, because if we're going to have a serious conversation, it's going to be when he's in his human form, even if it takes me a few hours to regain the strength after the fire test. Lysander has healed the wounds I had, and I'm mostly on the mend as I curl up on the sofa, a fluffy silver blanket draped over me from Grayson. Terrin's guilt is written all over his face as he comes off the balcony fully clothed in a dark grey shirt and jeans. But worse, I feel it in my soul, like it's my own emotion and it's eating me up inside.

Lysander is leaning against the wall by the

balcony, his gaze watching Terrin like a hawk. Grayson is sitting on the edge of our bed with his legs spread, and Arden is by the fireplace, tired but alert for whatever Terrin has called us together for. He wanted them here, and that alone tells me it's important, whatever secret he has been keeping. A part of me feels betrayed that he kept any secret from me. All the kings, in different ways, have kept something from me, but Terrin? It felt like there was never anything between us, and it was easy from the moment we met in terms of our hearts. We only had to fight the physical problems we had with him being trapped in dragon form.

Terrin takes the seat next to me on the sofa and offers me his hands, which I slide my own into, enjoying the heat of his touch and how it sends sparks down my body. "I'm going to tell you everything that I've not said. I didn't mean to keep anything from you, but it never seemed like the right time recently. We can go and see the tsar downstairs and my sister and tell them everything when you're ready. Because this changes everything."

"Changes what exactly?" Arden questions.

"It will be easier if no one interrupts me with questions till the end."

"Like fuck are we doing that. Just spit it out, and if you hurt her, I will beat the shit out of you —" I glare at Lysander and he pauses in his threat, one I know Terrin isn't taking seriously or addressing at all. "Fine."

"Terrin, I trust you." I straighten my shoulders. "But get talking."

"From the beginning…" He looks at the fireplace. "The castle, I'm going to start there. Its name is Lares and its soul-tied, like mates, is Hestia."

How does he know the castle's name? "Who are Lares and Hestia?"

"Hestia is a Greek goddess that came to this world a millennium ago. She actually lived in hell for a while, from what I understand of her history and her fate. She grew stronger there, and she came here with a part of the darkness from hell itself, Lares, except for that darkness was destroying this world and she couldn't send him back. Hestia couldn't part from it because it was her one true love, a man made of a darkness so never-ending, and she was his opposite. A light that never ended.

They decided, in order to save this world, to cast a spell on them both. She became part of this castle, part of this land, and the darkness itself became the castle. They are together, forever, and immortal here." I don't know what this has to do with us, but it's interesting, nonetheless. "Hestia has another name, the Matron."

My eyes widen. "Matron is a goddess?"

He nods once. "Yes, but she has no power left. All her power was merged into this place to make sure that it didn't destroy everything to hold the darkness down below, to hold the castle in place. I know this because Matron used the darkness to come and take me as a baby to save me because I am a direct descendant of them. They had a child thousands of years ago, and the darkness watched our family line all the way to me. They took my sister later on too, and we were brought up here, with you and your parents, until the Spirit Court was lost."

My heart is racing, and I don't know what to ask first. The kings are silent, and I don't blame them one bit. "Save you from what? Why take you?"

"Our parents. They were experimenting with evil magic. Using pregnancy and evil magic to

146

try to create powerful children. It didn't always work. I had four siblings before me, and they all died. The pregnancy and the magic would kill them. I was the first one that was born alive, but they didn't stop their experiments. They tested on me. I don't remember this, but a part of my soul does. I know, when the matron told me everything when I was younger, it was true. They had another child after me, and the matron claimed they were kind to that one. He had no magic, nothing like me, so they kept him to be an heir. Then they had my sister, and for a while they were kind to her too. They had another son not long after."

Terrin. I squeeze his hand. "So, it was only you that they hurt? I'm so sorry."

"Don't be sorry. Listen to the rest first. Then they started being cruel, but only to my sister for some reason. She started showing signs of magic, of dark magic, and Matron sent the darkness to grab her. My parents might not have missed me, but they went mad looking for her, so wrapped up in their quest to find their missing daughter that they ignored their other two children and left them to it."

A missing child. A girl. It all sounds familiar

to me, but it's Grayson, who pays more attention to everything happening than anyone I know, who figures it out. "You said heir. Only royals need heirs and would have the money, power and more to do what you say. There is a missing princess of the West, and she was taken. I believe you are telling us who you really are, Terrin."

"Are you…" I stand up and straighten. "Are you trying to tell me what I think you're saying?"

He nods. "I'm the royal heir to the West. The first tsar to be born. Downstairs in the dungeons is my brother, and yes, the commander was my brother too. My sister is the missing princess of the West." A silence echoes around us that makes my skin crawl, and I don't know what to make of it, but how could he keep this from me?

"That's a really big secret to keep, Terrin. How could you not tell me?" I get mad and my words rush out. "You knew the whole time when we were in the West, and you said nothing!"

He shakes his head and reaches for me. I can't pull away from him, not Terrin, not my mate. "I didn't know the whole time. I only remembered recently, when I came back to the castle here after being in the other world. Something snapped in my mind, and my memory came back. I should have told you straight away, but I hadn't gotten my head around the idea yet. I didn't want to add any more pressure when it changes nothing between us. I had no idea my brother and sister would come here so soon and have power."

"I kept the past from him and gave it back when he needed to heed the call of his blood and be the king of the West. Ayiolyn is to be united under your rule, all six of you, and this prophecy has played out for a very long time." We all turn to see Matron standing next to the wall. I don't know how she got in here, but she did. I look at her differently now that I'm aware she is a goddess and is in a weird relationship with the darkness below, which has killed my ancestors.

"Why didn't you take all of them? If you knew that they were being abused, why not take them all from the West?" Arden asks. "Why only Terrin and the sister?"

"It takes a great deal of magic for my

blessed darkness to travel across a great distance to save a child. We did our best. I knew that bringing him here, closer to his destined mate, would give him a chance to be a better person than his parents were, and it came true. Everything went wrong, of course, when the court fell, and everything changed, but he is now the rightful tsar—or king, as you might put it—to the West. It is time you unite the dragons and riders to stop this war before slaughter happens that no one will recover from. Cronus's army will go out there and slaughter every dragon and rider simply for following their king because they do not know another exists. You are the king of the West. You are the rightful one that I brought up to make sure is a good person, because the West needs a ruler who will choose peace and magic. Magic has been feared for too long out there, and dragons have been hidden away. It's had a long line of tyranny, and that will end with King Terrin of the West and the Dragon Riders."

We all look at Terrin, and I don't know what to say. The title rolls over me though, and somehow, it's perfect. Terrin has been a leader for the shadow dragons, and the others do look up to him. The riders will bow and bend for him if he tells them the truth, and the dragons will stop this fight.

We could take out Aphrodite's army together and win. I want to find a way to save Aphrodite's spelled army and all the innocents she has control over, but I don't believe they are people I can save anymore. They are already dead in every sense. Terrin explained to me how they haven't eaten or drunk water since they were spelled by Aphrodite, and their minds are gone by now. They are walking zombies with only one task— kill us.

Lysander leans off the wall. "Right, but there is a crowned tsar downstairs. Not being funny, but if we kill him, it solves our problems, and you get a shiny crown along with his army."

"He's my brother, he doesn't die," Terrin growls.

Arden comes to Lysander's side. "He attacked Elle and brought an army here, killing hundreds of your mate's people. Where does your loyalty stand?"

"He made mistakes, but he's been enchanted by Aphrodite's magic!" Terrin roars at them both. I grab his arm. "He's lost a lot, but he has a child and wife to go back to. Breaking the spell with Aphrodite's death comes first and then—"

"Then what?" Lysander challenges. "We need the dragons and riders to fucking stop the war, and waiting is fucking crazy."

"Enough," Grayson shouts, and we all turn to him in shock. "Lysander, Arden, you are asking him to kill his family. We don't do that shit, and it's wrong. I believe speaking to the tsar first is the best way to go and then see where we go from there. He will be punished for this attack if it's what he chose without Aphrodite's magic guiding him. I doubt it." He looks at them. "We have all been under her magic, and it's not easy to control. We give him a chance."

"Everyone deserves a chance." They look at me and I stare up at Terrin. "And as fucked up as it is, we try because it's you. The only part Lysander is right about is the dragons and riders. We need them to know and see you are enough to make them turn their dragons around and leave this war."

"And your sister?" Arden asks. "I don't believe it is safe to let that dragon free."

"She thinks you killed her brother for no reason, and she got her memories back sooner on her own," Matron adds into our tense conversation. "I chose to save her because, deep down, she has a good soul, and she could be a force of good in this world."

"Perhaps when she learns the true reason, then she can be calmed?" Terrin asks me, and I nod. I don't want to ever think of that day, and I still have nightmares of it. I think I always will do, but eventually his face will fade, and he will be nothing to anyone. I will make sure no one remembers him.

I lean up and cup his face. "No secrets. No more of this bullshit. We are one, and your battles are mine; your family is mine and mine is yours."

He kisses my palm. "I made a mistake and I'm sorry."

"I know." I lean my head on his chest and breathe in his smoky scent. I wonder if he will ever not smell like dragon and fire, and I kind of hope not. It's Terrin. He is my mate, and apparently one of my kings. The matron has disappeared when I look back, and I'm not surprised.

Arden walks over and opens the door,

swinging it out. He winks at me. "Elle, looks like you have a particular taste—you know, in kings."

I groan, walking past him, and he tickles me. I pout at him. "That's really not funny."

The others are laughing though, and I end up chuckling as Arden chases me down the corridor, the others close behind, only for us all to come to a sudden stop. At the top of the stairs is an earth guard with a dagger pressed through his chest and armour, holding a letter in place. The colour drains from my face, and Grayson walks over slowly, going to his knees. He closes the guard's wide, dead eyes and whispers words in Latin to him before pulling the note off his chest as I kneel at his side. I rest my head on Grayson's shoulder, quietly waiting for him if he needs anything from me, at his own pace. He is cold and shaking as he reads the note and tells us all what the pink, blood-stained letter says. "He was a childhood friend who I cared for, and he had two young children. His name was Paul. The note calls for me to come tomorrow at dawn, alone, to my court, from Aphrodite. First my sister, now him? I'm going to enjoy killing her."

I look at the man and back to my mate, anger burning in my chest like a flame. "I'll enjoy helping you. It's nearly over for her, and she is going to regret every life she took in our world."

CHAPTER 10

GRAYSON

I think about the beautiful mate I left in bed this morning, because saying goodbye to her isn't ever happening again. I never want to say goodbye to her. How do you say goodbye to someone who completely and utterly owns every inch of your body? I step through the portal, straight back to my court, and the earth beneath my feet feels like home. The earthy smell of the air, the dirt under my boots, and the tall trees blocking out the sunlight from the rising sun over the tips of the mountains. Home is an odd feeling for me, it was a place I once hated, and then it was a place I loved when I grew older, when I learnt that the land didn't hurt me and it was a good place. The earth is calm and peaceful—exactly what I have always needed to calm myself down when all I can see is darkness.

Aphrodite is waiting by a cavern entrance, not far from the mountain city my mate loved. The first time I fucked her was above that city, and maybe it's a sign of good luck Aphrodite chose this place. No Emrys with her this time, to my disappointment. He is in there; I fucking know it, and I keep seeing my mate's face every time she looks at Emrys. It is killing her that she can't save him yet. It's killing all of us, and these fucking tests are the only way for us to figure out a way to fix this all.

The orange sunlight flickers into my eyes as I approach the intruder not only to my court but to this world. I can still taste death in the breeze, carried from the Air Court and the slaughter she led. The bitch still has my sister locked away. My innocent sister. Her eyes drift down me, and I want to throw up all over her tight red dress. "King Grayson. In my boredom, I looked at the royal paintings, and you are by far the most handsome earth king ever to reign."

"I'll send your congratulations on to my

mate, who enjoys my face very much," I coldly drawl. "Get on with it."

Her eyes tighten in annoyance, and she brushes her long hair over her shoulder. "It begins for you here. I know you care about your people deeply, as deep as this earth goes in this region. This test is simple, easy even. Earth was always my favourite element. Go in and get ten people out alive." The way she smiles tells me it's not that simple.

"Just ten people?" I cautiously ask.

She swirls her hair around her middle finger. "Yes. They're in this section of the city. It's easy."

I wish she would stop talking. "Fine."

One step. I only take one step before her laugh makes me pause. "Well, I should say more, or it's mean. I don't like being mean to men who will be mine." I'd rather cut my dick off. "See, you have to touch and hug the ten people, and if you let go of them before they're outside the city, then they die."

I don't know what is worse. The idea of being anything to her or letting ten strangers near me. The thought of touching ten people sends a sickness rising up my throat and a cold shiver down my spine. It's different with Elle and it's different with the kings because they are family to me, but it took years for me to let them even pat my shoulder. Elle…she breezed into my life and made herself a rock, one I couldn't live without touching. The fear faded with Elle. She made it that bit easier to get over the feeling that locks my body up and makes me weak. Aphrodite has been in my head, and she fucking knows this. She knows what happens to me, how a touch from a stranger can throw me back to the boy being hurt by his mother. I clamp my teeth down hard enough that I feel like my jaw's going to snap in two. "Fine."

She points at the opening. "Oh, and you don't have long. I'll give you an hour. I'm being generous after my win in the last test. We both know that you'll maybe not win this, but if you do get to the end, I'll reward you by not slaughtering the people you save."

"Why?" I question.

She assumes I mean why is she being "generous." I meant why is she a psychotic bitch. "Earth was always my favourite element. I had parents once. I wasn't created out of nothing. They were called Druids, and they worshipped elements, which in turn gave them certain powers. They were connected to the earth around them. I grew up in a place like this, where everything the earth created was a blessing, except for their love. They loved each other deeply, viciously, and it tore them apart. I was caught in the crossfire of that. You know what having parents like that is like, don't you?"

"Stay out of my head," I growl, my dragon roaring in my mind to let him out and let everything burn. I'm tempted. "If your parents could see you now, would they be proud of you for destroying an element they loved? Taking a world that you're trying to destroy? Aphrodite, goddess of love. Maybe love destroyed you after all. Maybe their love did, or maybe you were just born evil."

Her eyes sharpen. "I'm going to very much enjoy breaking you. Have fun."

I don't give her the reaction or attention she wants; I just walk through the portal, straight down the steps towards the city. The longer I spend here is just more chance for her to piss me off and make me go after her, when I know deep down that would risk my sister and Emrys.

The wetness in the air should really have

given away what I was walking into, but still, it's a shock to see. My city is in a mudslide. Mud is cascading through the buildings at the bottom, spreading right down around the city in a fast current. It looks deserted, but apparently there are ten people here. All the cities were evacuated a while back, and my people are in hiding. There weren't many I trusted to stay and guard the castle and protect my sister.

I put my hands out and crack my neck before reaching for the earth, for my powers, and letting my magic soar. I let my senses explode around me, connecting me to the very earth under my feet. A vivid green light bursts before my eyes as I stop the mud, stop the very direction it's flowing, and I turn it to rock. It's a temporary fix. The force of the mud coming down will push the rock out of the way in time, but I will have more than an hour. I glance at my neat clothes and sigh. I like this shirt, but fuck it. The mud is tough as I walk down a few steps and right into it, but puddles of mud soon splash over me as I carry on.

This is going to be a bitch to fix this mess when I get my court back. I might need Lysander, even if asking that bastard to help with anything is a bad idea. "Hello!" I shout loudly. "Call out for help!" Nothing echoes back, nothing comes back except the sound of my shout, and the only sound I can hear is the rock cracking deep below my feet. I walk further in, up to the first building, or what is left of it. I don't have time to do anything but check as much as I can. The bottom two layers are completely gone. The once beautiful room is now nothing but mud and broken shit. I focus on a statue half buried in the mud at the back of the room, a llama in gold that glows brightly, even caked in mud. My mother used to make statues, and this is one of the few remaining. I remember her brilliantly designing them and being covered in dust and clay stuck to her clothes. She always created animals, always ones that she remembered from when she was a child or ones she had come to love in the court.

I'm not a believer in fate, but for this to be here, when this entire test is about the fear I got from her…it's hard to look away. That's when I see it. A red light shining from the vent. It's glowing dimly, but the statue catches the reflection of the light to make it more obvious. I climb in through one of the broken windows, following the light, straight through one of the rooms where the mud has gone so high that I practically need to crawl when I get towards the back of the room. I use my magic to make a pathway, careful and slow, in case someone is trapped.

The more mud I move, the brighter the light glows until I spot it—a magical sphere floating in the air—and inside it is a little boy. He's not so little, maybe eight or nine, but still a kid with dark brown hair that matches the mud, and darker skin. His clothes are clean and have the court symbol on his chest. He must have parents that work in the castle. When I get closer, the sphere vanishes around him, and the boy starts screaming in pain. I remember what the bitch said about needing touch, and even when it feels like spiders are crawling across my skin, when it feels like too much, I go over, and I pick the boy up. His screaming instantly stops.

"It felt like burning!" he sobs. "Please don't let that happen. It hurt. Did you do it? It stopped when you picked me up." The boy is like a monkey, wrapping his arms around my neck and never stopping his chatter so I can talk. He is shaking from head to toe, though, and it gives away that he is scared out of his right mind. "Where's my mum? I want my mum. I want my dad."

"Who's your mum and dad?" I question.

"Armel Derocles and River Derocles. They are royal guards, and I was with them and…" He leans back and he really looks at me, his eyes widening and colour draining from his face. "You're the king! I've seen a painting of you, and my mum told me you're in trouble. That's why you had to go fight for us."

"I'd never abandon my court and my people." I smile at him as he leans back to look at me. I still want to drop him immediately and scrub my skin raw from his touch, but I won't do that. I won't let my fear hurt this kid. I'd rather feel sick to my stomach and continue to keep him safe. "Unfortunately, we are in a test where our lives are in danger. You need to be grown up for me, and I'll get you back to your mum and dad, okay?"

"Okay." He's still crying, though. I remember being his age, just a scared little boy once. I remember what Elle told me, what she told me over and over. Every time she held my hand, every time she pushed past the barriers that I've had put in place for so long. She told me I'm brave, and fuck, I want to be for her. I know my fear is irrational—this youth wouldn't even be able to hurt me—but the irrational fears in my mind can be more powerful than any weapon I've held in my hands. "I'm Derrick, by the way."

I keep the boy in my arms and carry him to the main room, only putting him down by the statue. "Well, Derrick, call me Grayson. I'm worried if I let go of your hand, that pain's going to happen again. You need to hold my hand, okay? The pain will start if I let go of you. If I have to use my powers, I want you to go to my back and put your hand on my back. Do not let go as I defend you. Do you understand?"

He nods. "But why, King Grayson?"

I gulp and look into his blue eyes. "I don't like to be touched by strangers, and so the goddess who took you, and the others we need to find, thinks I'd be too scared to hold you, so she'd win this test, and I'd fail. What she doesn't understand is the woman who is my mate. She doesn't understand that my mate is who I'm doing this for, and my love for her overturns any fear."

He nervously grins. "I heard she is pretty."

A laugh escapes me. "Any other older boy said that, I'd be mad at them, but yes. She is very pretty."

He laughs with me for a second, but he still looks terrified. I don't blame him. I'm glad I made him smile. I never really liked kids, now that I come to think about it. But a kid with my eyes and Elle's face, maybe a boy like him? Fuck yeah. I want that. I have to work on convincing her when I get back. I want years with her first, but the idea of putting a baby in her, yeah, I can definitely get on board with that.

We work our way through the towers, through the small little huts where you can only just about see the rooftops before we find people along the way. Two women, both elderly, who hold on to the boy's hand and make a line behind me. As long as I hold on to one of them, it's fine, but I have to touch them first, so I hug each one of them, just pushing back every time against the sickness in my throat.

We find three young men, guards that I don't know, but they are a bit thrown by me, hugging them out of the blue and demanding that they hold on and make the line, but they listen to their king. They are all scared of dying, and they know being stupid is exactly going to cause that. After two more people, we find the final one, a woman about in her thirties, who says she was a cook in the palace and is equally terrified. A clicking sound echoes loudly. We all go still before I lead them out of the room and towards the sound.

"What's that noise?" Derrick questions.

I'm not lying to him. "I don't know, but I will not let anything happen to you." I step out of what must have been a storage room, maybe a barn, before the mudslide. I look up just to see another wave of mud bursting out over the top of the mountain. The clicking sound was the rock breaking above. My eyes widen as I let go of the boy's hand, feeling the boy's hand landing straight onto my back instead. I call my power like I never have done before, and even then, I don't know if it will be enough. I spread my hands out in front of me, my arms wide. My dragon roars from within me, making the entire world hear as the mud slams into us and I barely hold it back. They all scream, and I want to scream with them. The force of it is so great I nearly stumble into Derrick, and I grit my teeth, pushing against it, knowing they're all dead if I fail. I will not let my people die. I will not lose this test. The muddy water doesn't stop, and it isn't my element to control. My body starts glowing green, brighter than any light, as I touch depths of my power I haven't before.

I dig my feet into the ground as everything goes dark and there is just us, just my body glowing with a forest green light. "I am your king!" I roar, thinking of Elle. Imagining her. "And you will bend for me."

I feel a warmness to the air, a sweet, familiar perfume smell as everything pauses. Time slows softly, the mud parting just in front of me. Through the darkness of the muddy water appears a woman and a man. Both of them are glowing in the same green light as me. My parents. I watch them quietly as they come closer. In my mother's hands, a crown forms. The crown is stunning and calls to me like no object ever has. I don't like seeing her again and I do, all at the same time. It's fucked up. My mother walks to me, and on instinct, I bow my head. She places it on me, her fingers running down my cheek, and I flinch. Power flows through my body from the moment the crown rests in my hair, and I look up, seeing my father bowing. I look at my mother, who is fading before my eyes. "Goodbye."

She smiles, like I remember her smiling before everything went wrong, and I tell myself to remember it. To never forget that smile and try to think of it instead of the rest of our past. I quickly use the mud under our feet, making something akin to a bridge and lifting it high into the air, using force to push through the muddy water. They all scream as I grab onto the boy's hand and the green light spreads around him and down each of the people that I found, people that are alive.

I guide us towards the rock wall. They scream even louder, thinking I'm going to crash them into it, but it just breaks away right in front of me under my power, from simply a look. I've never been this powerful, and fuck, did it come at the right time. Lysander has his crown, but Arden didn't get one, so I wasn't expecting it. We come out into the sunlight, the darkness left behind us, and I take us down to the ground. The bridge breaks into dirt under their feet as I land, and let go of the boy's hand and wink at him before one of the women takes his hand and leads him away.

Aphrodite is waiting, a portal open at her side and the spirit castle on the other end. She's furious and I'm glad. "Where the fuck did you get that crown from? Why do they keep appearing?"

I look behind me to see my people running away straight towards one of the other cavern entrances to another part of the city. She made a promise not to hurt them, but I'd rather they were out of sight before I leave. I wait until they're gone before I bother to answer Aphrodite. "Because you're facing kings, you're facing a power you don't even understand. We have a whole host of ancestors that all want us to win because this is our world. So, as I believe my brothers have told you, get the fuck out of my court."

I walk through the portal, and I don't bother looking back. I won that test, and I won it for my mate.

CHAPTER 11

"*E*mrys," I whisper. It's him again. We are in the same place as before, this strange dream place that almost feels familiar to me. He's standing on a boat in the sea that looks like fog. It's so familiar, but I can't put my finger on where I've seen it before. Pretty though. I watch it slowly float, even when there are no waves or current. The water doesn't move. I walk through the fog-like water that just parts around my legs. Emrys offers me a hand and I step into the boat. We stare at each other, and he is smiling. Not as big as my smile, just before I throw myself into his arms, hugging him tightly. I can't smell his scent here. It's unnerving and I miss him. The real him. He holds me back, and he doesn't let go. "You came back."

He leans only slightly away from me to cup my face, his hands tucking my hair behind my ears. "There isn't any place in any world that I wouldn't come back for you, Elle. It's time."

My mouth parts. I want to kiss him, be with him, but he seems serious now. "What is time? If you're telling me it's time for you to die, we are going to have a big disagreement." I'm so scared of that thought I can't stop talking. "We are doing the tests. We are fighting for you, and I need you to hold on. Please, just please don't go. Please, I'll beg. I'll do—"

He kisses me, his lips pressing on mine before parting them. I melt into his touch, my eyes closing, and I let myself be lost in Emrys. "You need to go into the darkness below. It's time."

I shake my head. "I can't. You're not with us now. It could rip me apart and kill us all."

"Do you really believe I need my body to be with you?" he questions, covering my heart with his palm. "Our souls are one and you can call me any place, any time. I will always be with you, and so will they. You don't need your mates to go down to the darkness, and you do not need them to be crowned Queen of Ayiolyn. You were born to claim that title, and you already have your mates. It all waits for you in the darkness, and fearing it will end us all first.

"We are bonded to you. We always have been since our births. I can see it all now." He looks around us, and I see nothing but fog in every direction. "You can call them from down in the darkness to complete the mating when you're ready. You can call me too. I am yours now, to the end of our time, and even if there's only an inch of my soul left in existence, I belong with you. I always will do. It is time, Ellelin, to be braver than you ever have been. To face what is coming. This is the only day you will get before you face the final test that she has planned for you. You must have all the powers, or you'll die."

He is scaring me. "How do you know this?"

He strokes my back with his hand. "When your soul is not fully connected to a body, you wander and watch." He searches my eyes. "Don't be scared. I haven't let go yet."

Yet. Yet. Yet. I hate that. "Emrys…"

"It's going to be okay. Don't look so heart-broken. But wake up and face it for us. Grayson will win his test; I am sure of it. In the mean-time, you need to go down to the darkness alone. It is yours to face. It always has been. Without the others. They will stop you and they do not understand. I did not until now. Only you were born in the darkness and shadows. Only you can command them. I've seen it. I under-stand now." He soothes me with more madness. "Trust me, Elle. Do as I ask."

I can't catch him as he steps away from me. It feels like he's fading away with time, and no matter what I do, I won't be able to grasp him back. I scream his name, but it's too late. He is in the fog, and I can't see him anymore.

I wake up in a cold sweat and there's sunlight pouring through the windows, right into my face until everything is a bright yellow. "Gray?" I look around for him. We went to bed together last night. I wanted to spend as much time as I could with him before the test. Arden went back to his court to deal with some business there. Lysander was with his brother and Arty, making preparations for their mating, or marriage. Gray kept me up all night, happily, until we both collapsed and fell asleep. "What the air king claimed was true. Are you ready?"

I sit up straight and blink a few times because this can't be real. The matron is actually sitting in a chair by the fire, near the end of my bed. The flames of the fire are casting bright orange lights across her dark cloak. Her cloak covers her face, and her stick is resting over her legs. She looks at home and she hasn't even bothered to glance my way. "What are you doing in here?"

"Waiting for you to receive Emrys's message. It's time to escort you to the darkness." She finally looks at me. "And I've waited to bring you."

Not at all creepy. "I need to talk to my mates about it first—"

"They can stop you or demand to enter at your side. You were interrupted once before, and if you hadn't been, the darkness would not have let them in either way. They do not understand. Their blood doesn't run deep in the generations of fifth court royals. It is not their element. You are the princess of spirit. You are the princess of darkness and the very essence of it. If you do not go, then you die."

She has thought this through, then. It feels wrong to not tell them where I'm going, and it's not something I want to do. "I could die down there. It's killed my ancestors."

Her voice carries through the air. "That was because they were not chosen or invited. You are both."

"Did they know that?" I lean forward. "Did my grandparents know, or did you lead them down there?"

"Yes, they knew, and I advised them not to enter. They were grabbing power that was not rightfully theirs. Everyone's soul is tested in the darkness. Only someone who wants the best for this world, who deserves it and has been chosen, will be able to access his power." She speaks with clarity, but I don't understand this all, and something screams in my chest to tell the others. But if she is right, they won't let me go in there, and I won't be able to save my people. I won't be able to save everyone. This castle has always looked after me and been kind. It sang songs to me and got me out when the court fell. It saved me over and over, and likely more times than I know. I might not trust her, but the castle? I trust this castle with my life.

I've been spooked since Terrin told me everything and we went to see the tsar and his sister. Neither one of them said a word, like they had discussed this all and knew. But I could tell the tsar was shocked and pissed off. I know he didn't know about Terrin, even if he refused to show it.

I watch her. "You've been here, right? You saw my father go into that darkness. You saw him come out with that sword, which was from Cronus. He died."

For once, I actually see some emotion on her face. "Your father was a great man and a good king. He ruled well, and I liked him. I liked him enough not to let the darkness kill him and to offer him help instead, saving you and your mother. That's all he ever wanted. Did you know that? He just wanted you to live. A solution to his problems was what we gave him with that sword." We both glance at it, resting on the wall. "It's alive, as you well know, and it will aid you. It's a magical sword that is bursting with life."

I climb off the bed and walk over, stopping in front of her chair. I lean down so we are at eye level, noting how she smells like jasmine and winter nights. "You want me to trust you?"

"Did I not save your mate when he was only a boy from a life of cruelty that would have shaped him into a monster, a monster not even you could have saved? Did I not play the events to make sure that you were chosen and brought here? Chosen and brought here so that you could meet your other mates to free your mother to begin this quest. All of this hasn't just played out but has been shaped by me. Trust that this castle and I have kept you alive, kept you on the right path for a very long time." She offers me her hand, turning it over. In her palm is the Spirit Court crest. "I am bound to this court, and I would choose nothing different. I want not to rule but live in this castle in peace. To guide and watch the rulers of this world, but never be the ruler. I vow on my powers and immortal life."

"But why me? Why am I this chosen person? I never asked for this. I never wanted it."

"You were born to it, Ellelin, and the power in your veins is nothing short of the power that makes gods." She sighs and rises to her feet. "I have seen four futures for you. Four different futures, and only one of them is a fate you will survive. Two of them depend on you coming with me."

"Risk my life, not tell my mates, and believe you can see the future?" I question. "I do not keep secrets from them and risk everything!"

"You will soon be a queen of this world, and risking everything is a small price to pay. Yes, they are your kings and mates. That much is true, but you will be the queen of all elements. Only you will unite them. That does not come without risk or trust. If you do not trust me, then I will leave. If you do, then I will wait here while you get dressed. We will go to the darkness." She walks to the door. She pauses, never looking back at me. "The future I saw was happy. You were vacationing on Earth at Halloween, with your twin boys and mates. The twins were dressed up and collecting sweets as one more child brewed in your belly. There was peace in Ayiolyn under your rule, and a great elemental council presided over the courts, which were united for the first time. This future is waiting for you."

My heart is racing. "Wait!" I shout to stop her opening the door. I've never thought about having children before, but suddenly I want to hear what they would look like, what they might be like. Twins...boys. I don't know why, but something in my soul screams that it's right. "The twins...were they? I mean, tell me something about them. Please."

She touches the handle of the door. "Both of them have black hair and multicoloured eyes, which reflect the powers they have. One power from every court as they are the children of you all, magically bound." She walks out and shuts the door behind her, leaving me standing and watching nothing but my imagining of them. Imagining a future where I would feel safe enough to even have kids. I know it's completely and utterly mad to go with her into the darkness alone. The answers to releasing my people are down there, the magic to be able to do so.

"Your heart is racing. Are you well?"

Terrin's voice in my head makes me jump, and I know I can't tell him anything. "I'm fine," I lie even if it makes me feel sick to say it. "Just a bad dream."

"Come and ride. The fresh air will clear your mind," his soothing voice offers. Things are weird between us at the moment, and until now, I didn't realise what it is like to keep a big secret from my mate. I know deep down he did it because it wasn't the right time, but I hate that there is something like this hovering.

"I will soon. You know I love you and who you are. It changes nothing for me. You can decide whatever you want: be a tsar and rule, don't. I just want you and that won't change," I whisper back to him.

He is quiet for a moment. "I love you too. I don't know what I need to do, but with you at my side...we will find the answer."

"We will. Speak soon." I block him out as best I can. I know he'll be suspicious of that, but he'll stop me, and I can't control how I'm going to be scared. I choose some comfortable black clothes and go to the bathroom. My long-sleeve top sticks to me, and I tuck the end into my high-waisted, tight dark jeans before putting my boots on. I throw on a cloak, one hanging on the back of the door, because it might hide who I am for a moment longer.

Before walking out, I catch my reflection in

the mirror. My hair is down, falling in purple waves down my chest to my waist. My eyes sparkle blue and remind me of Lysander's element. I'm doing this for them. Before I get to the door, it opens. Instead of the corridor outside, it opens straight into the corridor at the bottom of the castle, right opposite the doors to the darkness. I glance at the matron standing next to the doors. "You're going to have to teach me that trick with the castle. It would make getting around a lot easier."

She flashes me a secretive smile, suggesting she will not be doing that. The doors to my bedroom slam shut behind me, and with a wave of her hand, all the doors lock, except for the ones in the darkness. "I will wait here until you return, princess, but you will come out as queen. The title *princess* ends. I will stop the kings from entering if I must."

"Do not hurt them," I warn her, and she nods once. "Tell them it was my choice and to wait for me. That I'm sorry."

My heart races as I go to the door. I feel like I'm being called here, like I have been called here since I was a baby. This dark place was waiting for me, and I've avoided it long enough.

The darkness. I straighten my back, standing in front of the doors, and grab the handles. I know everything will change when I go in here. Maybe I want it to be that way. I don't have enough power to save this world when actual power has been sitting down there in my castle the whole time. I turn the handles, and I push the doors, which open for me, revealing a cloud of glittering black dust. I feel like it wraps around me, pulling me inside. A scream echoes out of my mouth as I'm thrown forward into nothing but glittering black darkness that has no end, no smell and no feel to it.

I'm thrown to my knees, invisible pressure pushing down on my shoulders. My arms are yanked out in front of me, and the dragon marks on my wrist begin to glow the colour of the element they are from. The red dragon for Arden, my fire king. A blue dragon for Lysander, my water king. A silver one for Emrys, my air king, who I will not lose. The final one glows a vibrant green for Grayson, my earth king. A new one appears, right below Lysander's, a black glittering dragon marking outlined in yellow. The yellow and black glow for Terrin, my king of the West.

I drag my eyes up and around, looking at the moving fog that seems alive, like it's real and far more than a fog or darkness could be. The song of the fifth court starts playing, loud and humming. The beat vibrates the floor under my knees, and in the darkness, I relax. Slowly, a room starts to appear around me, the darkness fading away, until slowly, I realise I'm in a very plain room with white walls and dark black square tiles across the ground. There are no windows, no doors, nothing but the walls.

A man stands in the middle of it, a man who I wished I'd never see again, and instantly fears slams into my chest. The commander. He doesn't look right. He looks pale…and dead.

He's dead.

He holds a sword in his hand, and the force pushing my arms up and holding me in place disappears. I reach for my powers, but nothing happens. I have no one to stop me as he runs at me with his sword raised high, a battle roar coming from his mouth. I scream, barely rolling out of the way. He slams the sword straight onto the stone, and it clangs. I reach for my powers again, but they don't come. "Fuck." No powers, great.

The commander swings his sword at me again. This time, he hits me straight through my leg, and I scream as I fall onto the floor, blood pouring out of the wound. As he looks down at me, I freeze. I'm back on that bed, those drugs in my system, and I can't move. I can't fight him. I need my mates. I don't know why Arden comes to mind first, but he does. The minute I think of him, fiery flames appear in my hands, like they've been carried in on the wind for me to use. Arden's flames burst from my fingertips and blast over the commander. He screams and begs, but the flames take on their own life, burning and destroying, taking and taking until there is nothing but ash and dust. The sword clinks onto the ground in front of me. My eyes widen as I look down at my hands, the flames still rolling around my fingertips before dancing down my wrists and into the dragon there. The feeling of a fire burning hot through my blood is so different from my shadow power. "What was that?"

"You. You are connected to them all, Queen of Ayiolyn. You faced your greatest fear alone." The glittering darkness appears again. I see nothing more than a cloud of sparkling black dust in front of me, playing the fifth court song again and again, a haunting melody echoing in my ears, but I know it's a lullaby. It's our song.

I stare at the darkness, the magic bound down here, and how endless it actually is. It is pure power, like nothing I've seen or felt before. "Thank you for saving me. I was born here, and you never gave up on me, did you?"

"Never," the darkness whispers back, the male voice old and ancient. Soothing, like a grandfather speaking to his grandchild. "I saw your birth long before you came into my castle, kicking your little legs and screaming. You were prophesied to save the world I love. Ayiolyn. I did everything possible to save you and make sure you have a life, a future. What do you want?"

"I want a better world. I want a world where people are all free, united and equal. Earth has its problems, but in some places, it's like that. I think Ayiolyn can be the same. Everyone can have their magic; we can be united under one ruler. I want my mates; I want the future that I have tirelessly fought for, and one that I can have my children grow up in. Safe. You said I was chosen to unite this land, to make it better, and I felt like I couldn't do it. Now I realise I will do anything to make a world where men like him are not in charge. I was born here, in this castle." I smile at the darkness. "You're like a parent I didn't notice, and I'm sorry. I belong here with my family, and that is you, isn't it?"

The darkness was always my home. It moves to me, the cloud of sparkling darkness spreading around my body like an embrace. It's more than that, it's power. I feel the weight of the crown nestling in my hair, and the endless power that bursts throughout my body. I feel every bit of the castle. I find my mates and direct them to me. Terrin, I find outside and then my people. Each one has darkness wrapped around them, and it's easy enough to pull it away, one by one. I see them shift back into people, thousands of them, but they can shift when they want. My people of the Spirit Court. I leave Terrin till last, watching as the spell is broken on my mate.

"Connect to your elements," a male voice commands me, an ancient voice of power and darkness. A voice I will never forget. "Fire." Red fire shoots out of the wall, but I don't fear it. It's Arden. It's Arden in every way. The fire begins to slowly spin around me in circles. "Water." Blue water shoots out of the floor and does the same thing, spinning around, dancing with the fire almost. "Earth." A vine bursts out of the ground before wrapping in knots, before making circles, spinning in the air around the water and fire. "Air." A cold gust of air blows into the room. The silvery sparkling magic joins the circle until it's spinning around me so much that I can only just see the darkness.

"Darkness." The cloud itself spins, joining the elements, spinning around so fast my feet are lifted off the ground and I'm floating in the air as the darkness pushes and wraps tightly around all the elements, blocking out all the light before slamming them straight into me. I gasp, feeling the power burning through my veins, but it hurts. It feels like it's ripping my body apart and making it anew. I light up with each element, glowing from head to toe, and when I open my eyes, I see my mates. All five of them are standing in the room, the glow of my light across their bodies, and they are in awe.

One by one, they kneel and bow. Their crowns appear on their heads, one by one, the crowns I saw with my father. They each glow, and only Terrin is left without a crown, but he is glowing yellow. Gold almost. It's the darkness's voice that echoes. "Bow to the Queen of Ayiolyn, the elemental queen of the dragons."

CHAPTER 12

TERRIN

*E*lle kisses my cheek before leaving with her other mates. It's been five hours since she went into the darkness on her own and somehow bonded herself to it, becoming far more powerful than any ruling queen of any court. She has every power now, and it was an honour to be able to witness any of it. She was glowing with every colour of the elements, and they were bending to her will.

I don't remember the moment the dragon spell broke, but it snapped like a broken branch, and then I was standing with the others in that place. Time seemed to just stop, and after Arden mostly told her off for doing this alone, we just walked out together. I think they are all just as amazed as I am and so proud of our mate. She is ours, ceremony or not. We can have some royal ceremony to mark her as the queen if she wants, but I'm not fussed about any of that shit. I want her soul, her heart, and I don't want anything else. My mate looks back, her eyes finding mine. "Are you sure you don't want me to come with you?"

"I think it's better I do this alone. I'll find you after," I promise her. I can't speak in her mind anymore. That seems to be lost with the spell that bound me to my dragon form. "Go rest."

"We got her." Grayson nods at me and I nod back. I didn't like any of them to begin with, but they are growing on me. They are good men, and they only want to please Elle. Having that in common, we might even become friends.

I watch them go before turning and walking down to the dungeons. I'm going to go every day until they speak to me, until they finally listen. I don't know whether they've taken in anything I've said. I hope they did, but if they didn't, they're still my family. My sister, I've always had. Even in dragon form, we used to fly together. She was fine till she took the commander on as her rider. Did she know he was her brother? Maybe. Maybe that was when the obsession started. Maybe she can't understand why we killed him. I hate the thought of that motherfucker, and if I could have killed him a thousand times over, it wouldn't be enough. Fuck him.

I enter the dungeons, which are warm, and the castle has kept them nice. I look at my sister first. She's not in dragon form anymore. The spell was broken on her too, and I'm glad to see it. She's wearing a black cloak, her long black hair falling down her back, and she stares at me with the same colour eyes as mine. "The spell is broken. Well done. Now what do you want, brother?"

"I'm going to send you back to the West with our brother. Hate me if you want, but you're my family." I lift my chin. "And first you're going to make a vow in blood never to harm anyone from the Spirit Court, including Ellelin."

"She killed him!" she seethes. "He was your brother too, if what you're saying is correct, and she killed him. He was my rider!" Her eyes grow wet with tears.

"He was a rapist, and what else do you want me to say? She is my mate, but even if she wasn't, if I caught him hurting anyone like that, I'd have killed him!" I shout.

"I don't believe you!" she shouts back, but it's weak. She must have been able to sense his emotions towards Elle at the very least.

"Yes, you do, you're just too stubborn to admit it. You're siding with him because of that bond that's clawed into your chest, and with time, you will recover from the death of the bond and get your mind back. I know deep down you are a good person who has done terrible things. I felt the bond with my own rider and I know what it's like to have that deep connection to someone other than yourself. I've seen other dragons in the West lose their riders and become insane. They often chose to die, and nothing we said could save them. You remember this, and yet you're still alive. You chose to continue on with your life. He's dead and you've bonded with another rider. He's alive next to you. He's also your brother too, and so am I. Time will heal your soul, sister." I leave her and walk down to the tsar's cell.

The tsar looks like a broken man. Fuck, I

don't even know his name. "What's your name?"

"My family calls me Aodhan," he answers in an indifferent tone. Aodhan. All those years I've seen him in the West or heard of him through the whispers, and he was my family all along.

"I need something and I'm not bullshitting around the topic," I tell him outright.

"Do you expect me to give it to you?" he actually questions, coming into the light. We don't look remotely like each other. I don't think I'll quite get used to that. My sister, at least I see that we have the same eyes, but him? Nothing. "Do you know how insane our parents were when they were looking for her? They never mentioned you, not once. But her? The obsession with the missing princess, it never stopped. Never. It went on and on, and they blamed the East. Maybe they knew, and it's why magic became so hated and the war became what it is now. So much death on both sides, and now what? What do we do next?"

I cock my head to the side. "They were monsters, and maybe following their example is a path we can choose to avoid. We can be different."

"Yes, they were, but not to me. Maybe they would have been to you, I don't know. But they were evil to their people. I worked hard to stop that. My wife…she won't forgive me for what I did with Aphrodite. I didn't want to. No part of me wanted it. But I broke every vow we had anyway. I have nothing to go back to, and you might as well kill me. The land is yours then, and you can rule." He laughs, but it's hollow. "I have nothing."

Against my better judgment, I take the key, and I unlock the door. I sit down on the bench, feeling the cold seeping through my trousers. He surprises me by sitting next to me, and I watch him for a long time. "You won't know if she'll forgive you if you stay here, if you stay locked in here. Make a vow and tell me how to be the king of the dragons out there and the riders."

"You want to be tsar?"

"Whatever the fuck title you want, I don't care, but those dragons cannot attack with Aphrodite. They will die. We all will die. I need you to come with me and tell them I'm in charge." I lay out my plan.

He searches my eyes. "Why bother with me? Just kill me."

"You're family, and I don't give up easily. So, no." I slip my dagger out of my trousers. "Your hand, brother."

He lays his hand out, and I draw a line across his palm in blood. It's up to him now. "I vow on my blood never to harm anyone bound to the Spirit Court or Ellelin. I suspected what my brother was, but I never had any proof, and I loved him. My wife hated him, and she never said why. And now, now that I know the truth, I think, is there a reason why? Did she know? I've always been protective of my family, but I look back and only see failures."

He pulls a crown out of his cloak. "How did you get that in here?"

"It's bound to our blood," Aodhan explains. The crown is yellow, glittering. It's magic. "It's always rejected me. The crown's been in our family for generations, and our father could never wear it either. I don't know why I kept it close. I thought my child would wear it one day, but it wants you."

The minute I touch it, it glows brighter. I feel like it controls me as I gently rest it on my hair, and I feel the power from it spread through my veins, wrapping around sharp dark magic within my chest. "Thank you."

"You were destined to be a tsar or king, it seems, and I will not stand in your way. I just want to go back to my wife, to my family. I will take our sister with me." He looks at her. She is sobbing in the corner of her cell.

I rise to my feet and go to her cell, opening it next. I walk in and she looks up. "You're free, but you will never be welcome here, not after what you've done. Ellelin comes first. Make the vow before you leave with Aodhan soon."

Aodhan walks with me to the door, and he looks lighter, happier almost. "I never wanted to be tsar. I only wanted freedom."

Now he has it, and it is mine.

CHAPTER 13

I'm ready. We all are. I touch the crown nestled in my purple hair, the black crystals smooth under my fingertips before I lower my hand and find Terrin watching. A yellow crown sits on his head now, and it suits him. He was born to be a king of the West, and I owe Matron for making sure he got the opportunity to grow up how he did. I glance at my powerful mate for a second, noting how his crown is magical itself and gives him control over shadows, similar to my own gifts. Terrin leans down, his five o'clock shadow tickling my ear. "I won't let anything happen to you."

I know the sentiment is shared by all of my mates, even Emrys, who today is coming home.

I won't accept another ending to this test. Aphrodite sent word last night after the mating ceremony that the test would begin for me this morning at dawn. None of us slept or even attempted to. I trained with Gray, ate with Lysander and Arden, and oversaw our people with Terrin. Literally anything but attempting to sleep, when today is everything. We win or lose, and the other way, everything stops.

Arden, Lysander and Grayson are on my other side, and we are waiting for the sun to rise above the horizon and shine through the balcony of a clearing to the west of the castle. "I didn't tell you something, something I learnt from Matron." I feel the weight of their gazes on mine. "She can see in the future. I don't know how exactly it works, but she told me that I'd have twin boys. That we would take them trick-or-treating on Earth, something I always loved to do with Phobos. That is the future we're fighting for. When we step through this, Cronus is going to send his army out and defeat Aphrodite. The dragons have bent to Terrin, and his brother has returned to his lands to heal from the mental damage Aphrodite has done. It will take time to defeat an army that large, but the dragons of the West are on our side. When Cronus and my grandmother, along with Phobos, attack, the dragons will turn on Aphrodite's army too. They'll be attacked on either side. This is the last stand of the Spirit Court, and my court behind me will lead." Behind me stands Hope and Xandry, Arty and Kian, Livia and Jinks, along with a few Twilight priests, who are opening portals to the Water Court for healers.

"We will be free, along with all our people in every court," Arden adds in. "We have to beat her, kill her today, and get Emrys back along with the other hostages. Their safety is our goal."

Lysander claps his hands. "Kill some gods and then we can work on impregnating our mate. I love this plan."

My cheeks burn, and my eyes shoot to Lysander. Arden only high-fives him, and I shake my head at them both. Grayson's deep laugh echoes loudly, and his hand tightens in mine as he leans down. "Behave because the idea of trying to get you pregnant is making me hard, and you can tell me all about our future later on."

Warmness spreads through me. "I will."

I'm still nervous, but I hold my head high as I walk through the portal with my mates. My kings. We're all matching with thin black armour that is designed to fend off any elemental attack but also is good for effortless movement, like running. My magical sword is clipped to my back, and each of my kings is wearing a variety of clothing and weapons that makes them more impressive than usual. My mouth went dry when I saw them earlier, and I'm sure all the extra fluids in my body went right between my legs. The mate bond is still humming in my blood, and it makes me want them endlessly. I look behind me once to see that my court is watching us go. Each of them bows their heads, and it's the last I see of the Spirit Court, of my home, before the portal slams shut behind us.

The howling wind of the Air Court greets. It's a haunting song that sounds like it carries the ghosts of all the dead. It sends a chill straight down my spine, long before I see Aphrodite and Emrys. He looks worse, just so much worse. His skin's pale, almost grey, and it reminds me of ash in colour. There's nothing bright about him right now. His eyes are glowing, burning red, but they're flickering every so often. My heart races when I see that. Is Ares winning or is Emrys?

He's sitting on the throne, one that Emrys used to sit proudly in. But now he looks like a broken king, destroyed from the inside out, and it tears me apart to see him like that. I remind myself this will be over soon. I tell myself that Ares will get the fuck out of his body, and I will get my air king back. I have to drag my eyes over to Aphrodite, and looking at her just fills me with a burning anger. She's not wearing her usual dresses now; instead, she's wearing a tight, dark red suit that sticks to her curves, with a low dip in her chest. Her long blonde hair is down, and I very much look forward to yanking the strands of it out as I slowly kill her. I don't think I've ever wanted to kill someone as much as I do her. I've had enough. "Where's the final test?" I ask coldly, my voice carrying on the wind.

"Pretty crowns," Aphrodite coos, "but they won't save you. Your men can stay here. This is a test for women. Come."

I look into each one of my mates' eyes,

wishing we could communicate through our bond again. It would make this moment so much easier. I know they don't want to let me go. Grayson's hand tightens in mine before he is the first to let me go. His voice is a whisper for my ears only. "The only reason I can let you go right now is because I love you beyond all the fear. All of you. Go."

"Kill her." Lysander offers his advice. "And fuck, come out with her blood all over you. I don't care, but she dies."

Arden nods in agreement. "Come back alive, princess."

Terrin simply kisses the side of my head, like he can't find the words, and I don't need them from him right now. "If I don't come back out of there alive, kill Ares. Make sure they are both stopped, as she isn't coming out." Leaving my mates is more difficult than I thought it would be, but I only have to drift my eyes to Emrys to know it's worth it.

I reluctantly step through with her into an ancient, half-broken stadium with pillars stretched far away up in the dark sky. It smells like sand and people, and I'm not sure where we are. The air is humid but a little cold, and it's loud. Wherever we are, there is traffic near and a lot of people. Even though it's night, light shines down from electrical lanterns. Aphrodite waves around, dust picking up at her feet. "These are the long lost remnants of where I used to live. For a long time, your people worshipped me, and they would have done anything for me. And you, who have lived on this planet for so long, are here to kill me. Ironic."

"I suppose it will be ironic when you die here today." I draw out the *when*.

She laughs, shaking her hair off her shoulder. "The problem with Earth, and what I always found was a real issue, was those beating hearts inside the humans. That moral compass in your souls. You won't let people die, and that is exactly what will get you killed today." She is smug and confident. Maybe in her shoes, I would be too when I had no idea what I was facing. She waves her hand, and five doors appear. Literal stone doors with metal knobs stand in the middle of the stadium. The doors are all slightly different because they have a symbol etched into the stone on them. Fire, water, earth, air and darkness. The crests of the courts. "You will begin with the fire element because you loved him first. Then water, and so on. Darkness is left for last. Your task is to get through and survive each element within a limited timeframe of an hour. Sounds simple enough. You should thank me."

"Like fuck would I ever thank you," I snarl. Her comment about my heart and about my morals makes me think there's going to be people in there who are going to stop me from going through and make me want to save them. I will save them. Having a heart is not a weakness. "And overall, fuck you." I walk to the door with the fire symbol on it. "It turns out in all the years that you've been alive, you've still not figured out that you're pointless." I turn the handle of the door. Pure heat blasts at me from the other side. I look back at Aphrodite, and I swear she sees me for the first time. She sees the Queen of Ayiolyn, who will stop at nothing to save this world from her. "When I come out the other side of this, the first thing I'm doing is running my sword straight through your black heart to send you to hell. Ares will follow."

"We will see," she smugly replies. Fuck her. I step in and slam the door shut behind me. A small cavern stretches out with a cliff edge hanging over blistering fires. The fires are so hot they're burning blue, not red. There's a series of tiny pillar steps with enormous gaps between them leading all the way across on the other side, and there are three different paths. One straight across and one to the left. The path to the right is broken beyond repair and not usable. The stone door with the water crest on it is on the other side of the cavern where the paths meet, waiting for me.

"Help!" a female voice screams. Following the shout, I spot the outline of a woman sitting on the path to the left. There are more steps towards her too, but they are far smaller and far between. Fire, like a waterfall of it, is flicking all the way around her in a circle. It's getting closer to her by the second. She's screaming and crying, catching ablaze in places. I can only make out she is blonde.

"I'm coming to help!" I shout at her. What Aphrodite doesn't know, and what she's stupid enough not to have realised, is that I don't just have my shadow powers now. I pull water from the wall, using my powers to sense a deep ravine not far away. Grayson's powers make it easy to make a gap in the rock and lead it this way. Cold water bursts from the wall, enough of it that it soon pours out into streams, putting out the fire below, washing the waterfall of fire away into steam and ash. I jump over the rocks one by one, easy enough now that the flames aren't licking the edges of them, and get to her. I smile at the scared woman and offer her my hand. She must be about my age, and her accent is definitely British. "You're safe."

"What's going on? Where are you from? Why are you dressed like a queen with a crown?" she splutters. "Was that magic? Is magic real?"

She keeps going, and I let her blurt a million questions out before she bursts into a hysterical crying spell that I'm clueless how to stop. "I'm Ellelin, what is your name?"

"Soph," she sobs. "From Blackpool. I work in the arcades on the pier, and I…well, I saw something glowing and suddenly I was here. I was with three others, my friends and our manager!"

"Let's get you back to Blackpool, then, come on." I help her stand and I know she doesn't trust me, but I hope she at least follows.

I use Gray's earth power to make the path more structured, making a long path all the way across to the other door. The water symbol glows blue, and Soph looks terrified. Her jeans are burnt around her ankles, and parts of her pink crop top are black. "Stay close and you will live. If you run away, I'm not chasing you."

I mean, I likely would save her life, but I'm not telling her that. If she was the reason I could fail these tests, I'd leave here for Emrys's back. It's selfish, but it's true. My mates come first, and they always will do. Soph still follows behind me through the door, and it slams shut behind me. I'm not too surprised to see that we're underwater in some kind of bubble, barely holding the air in, and it is bubbling at the edges. There are sharks, thousands of them, angrily swimming fast and quick around us. I can barely make out anything through them. Pulling air from the surface of the sea high above, I slam it into the bubble until it is solid. Soph starts crying loudly, wrapping her arms around her legs. "I hate sharks!"

"That makes two of us," I mutter. Aphrodite chose this test to break me, and she won't win. Maybe with just my shadow powers, I might not have been able to save myself in here. The matron and Emrys were right. I needed the others. Lysander is king of the sea and all its creatures. I am his queen, and I can do this. I close my eyes, blocking everything out, and reach farther. I tell the sharks to leave. One word echoed from my mind into theirs. When I open my eyes, they are all gone.

The sea is glittering and clear underneath the surface, and right near the top in another one of these spheres of air that is slowly shrinking is a man. I move our air through the water, straight to him, before we crash into him. Our air bubble merges with him like I suspected it would.

"Who the fuck are you, and can you get me out of here?" he shouts.

"Don't shout at me, and calm down!" I warn him. He's a small bald man in a suit. The manager, I'd guess. His accent tells me he's from London without needing him to say. "Just stay close and you'll survive this." He goes to Soph's side, and she talks softly with him. He must be a good manager and not a sleazeball like my old one was.

I find the next door another twenty metres away in the water. It's easy enough to get us there and step into the air test next. This one is a bit more complicated. It's a massive tree spread high up in the air, but the tree is full of snakes. The same snakes from the first test, but some of them are massive. Aphrodite went all out to stop me. Such a shame I won't be climbing that. I'm missing two more people, Soph's friends, so I'll have to search for them on the way up. I still remember the pain from those snakes' teeth sinking into my body, and I hope the hostage here hasn't been bitten. "Both of you, stand close."

"We don't even know who you are and—"

"I'm Queen Ellelin of Ayiolyn, which is a world of dragons. I grew up on Earth and I'm trying to get us all out alive. If you want to die, then just stay here with the snakes. Want to live? Come close and don't move," I cut him off.

Soph touches his arm. "Think of your boyfriend. I'm thinking of mine, and we can do this. I think she is helping us."

He still doesn't look like he trusts me, but he comes closer with Soph. I lean down, making the ground around me shake before breaking away like a rock. I use my air powers to raise it straight up in the air and my earth gifts to hold it firmly together against the pressure. I don't need to climb the tree at all. I find another woman in a heap of black clothes and vibrant green hair, just about to be eaten by the snakes, and I use vines to wrap around her waist, yanking her onto the rocks. Soph hugs her immediately as I lift us up higher and higher. She's crying so much I can't understand a word she's saying, but I know I don't want to stay here for too much longer.

I land on top of the tree, in front of the door to the air test. This test has a tornado right in the middle of a clearing, and there is nothing but sand for miles. The new girl, who I think is called Molly, begins to scream. "No, no, no, no! I don't want to die!"

I glance at them and make a dragon out of shadows right underneath us. She loses it more, and I don't blame her. I meet Soph's eyes, the only reasonable one of them all. "Hold on."

She nods and does as I ask. The sooner I get them back to Earth, the quicker they will stop screaming. My shadow dragon spreads out far, and I realise I don't feel a drain on my power at all. Making a shadow dragon barely makes me flinch now. With a smile, one I hope Aphrodite can see, I fly us straight towards the fast grey tornado. I use my air powers to calm it, so the wind doesn't attack us as I fly straight over the top and down the centre with my screaming new friends. In the centre of the tornado is my last hostage to rescue. She's unconscious, and the moment I land, they all run to her. The other door is right behind her. The last one.

I yank it open, seeing the man picking her up with Soph and Molly's help to carry her after me. There is nothing but darkness waiting for me, and I know Aphrodite never expected me to get this far. This was the end. There's nothing here to attack me. I hold my hand out, and the door straight back to the arena opens in front of me. Aphrodite is shaking her head in disbelief, her mouth parted as I step through, the people coming in after me and running away. Not that I blame them. At least they got a free holiday to Greece.

"How did you do that?!" she roars at me, red power spinning out of her hands. I use the earth gifts to wrap around her ankles and hold her in place for me. The air whips around me as fire and water spirals out of my hands, taking on the shapes of dragons and running across the floor to her. She screams, her powers doing nothing against mine. "I won the test." I slowly walk to her. "I warned you about what was going to happen. I am Queen Ellelin, and you are no longer welcome in my world." I tug my sword from the clip at my back, and I plunge it straight through her chest, straight through her black bitter heart, just like I promised to do. I don't think death has ever felt as rewarding as it does right now. I watch her choke.

"Beautiful," the creepy sword whispers. That's enough of the sword for now. She shakes, grabbing onto the blade, cutting into her palms, but I pull it out, sliding it back into the holder. She collapses onto the dirt, blood spilling around her and into her hair.

"I don't have the humanity in me to sit down here with you while you die. You deserve to die alone on Earth and be forgotten. Just another unnamed dead for them to bury in silence." I raise my hand and make a portal to the Air Court. "Goodbye, Aphrodite."

Her scream is the last thing I hear as I step through the portal, and moments later, I feel my mates and the bond back. It was her spell that stopped us, and now...I just need Emrys back.

My heart is in my chest as I see Emrys first. He's holding my mother tightly, his hands around her neck, and she is grabbing the hand to pull it off with no luck. Gray's sister is in a cage right on the edge of the rock, the air barely holding it up using Emrys's power. I put my hands behind my back and make a ledge under the cage to catch the cage and make sure it doesn't fall when he no doubt lets go. A drowning man grabs anything and anyone to take with him. Ares is not taking another person from us. "I won the test. You have to get out, Ares."

"She made the test with you and she's dead now. I am not doing anything she agreed when you've killed her. You want him out? Make me!" he screams at me. My mates come close to me, and I lift my head. He is breaking a magical bond, a promise, and there is always a cost to that. I just didn't expect magic to take its price straight away. It does. Red, violent magic-like pulses start flowing out of Emrys's chest and tearing up the ground at his feet. My mother screams and he throws her to the side, her head smacking on the ground, and she passes out. Emrys screams and roars, holding his hands over his chest like he can hold in the soul. I want to run to him, but I can't get close, not with the magic throwing me around. Ares laughs. "When my soul is free from this body, I will take another and another. I will never be stopped. I am endless and there is no one who can take my soul and kill me."

I scream as his power slams into me, and the air becomes tight as it disappears around us. We all fall to our knees, gasping for air, and I reach for Grayson first as he stares at me, desperate to save me too. Terrin, Arden and Lysander are crawling to me even when they are going pale, even when every breath hurts. Ares is going to suffocate us long before he leaves Emrys and then takes one of our bodies. We can't stop him. I want to scream but nothing comes out.

Light shines and I roll onto my back, looking over as a new portal appears. Arty and Kian walk through it, hand in hand, and they aren't affected by the power. It bounces off them, disappearing altogether, and Arty's eyes are glowing like diamonds, her hair bouncing around her shoulders. They walk between us, almost like the magic can't touch them, like it's siphoning itself into Arty. It's her power. She leans down in front of me, and she kisses my cheek. "You were the sister I always wanted, and this is my choice. Don't you dare cry for me and maybe, maybe you can tell your family one day about your best friend who...who loved you."

That sounded like a goodbye. I can't speak, I can't breathe. I reach for her, trying to grab her hand and stop this. I don't know what she is doing, but she is not saying goodbye to me. I sob as she looks at me with tear-soaked eyes and rises off her feet. "It was always meant to be like this. I was their downfall. Ares created his own ending with me."

Kian leans down to say something to Lysander, touching his head for a moment. I don't know what it is; I don't know what he says, but whatever it is, I feel it from Lysander. A slam of emotion, a mixture of grief, shock and pure denial. Arty and Kian walk together straight up to Ares, and they take his hand. Ares shakes his head, trying to rip his hands from them, but neither of them let go. "Go to hell, dad."

Red light slams into both of their bodies, and it shines through their veins, bursting out of their bodies as Emrys is drained of Ares once and for all. Emrys collapses on the floor. The light swirls around them both, red and violent evil, but they hold each other as it stops. The world goes darker than it's ever felt. Everything stops as Artemis and Prince Kian die together for Ayiolyn.

CHAPTER 14

There's silence, where not even the wind dares to make a sound, where nothing moves as I look at what has just happened, and I can't believe it. It doesn't feel real to me, and I blink like it might make it all stop. Like they all might get up and this isn't real. The denial makes me feel sick to my stomach, and pain slams into my heart. Kian and Arty have collapsed together, their bodies entwined in each other's on the floor, and both of them are pale, still. Emrys is behind them, looking just as pale and just as dead.

Emrys.

I can't feel him. Panic floods my system as I realise I can't feel him. I thought…I thought the bond would kick into place. Grayson looks right at me before he runs for his sister, and I finally make myself move even if I don't feel connected to my body from the shock. Lysander moves with me, both of us running to the group. He grabs his brother, and I find my mate, hating the fact he doesn't move.

"Kian, don't you fucking do this to me! WAKE UP!" Lysander roars, storm clouds bursting across the sky and rain pouring down on all of us. Drenching us to the bone. Lysander sends water all over Kian's body, but it doesn't glow, it doesn't heal him. It can't, because there is nothing to heal anymore. Lysander has lost his brother, and I lost my best friend.

Arden looks down at Lysander. "I'm so sorry. They used their souls, their very essence, to kill Ares, and nothing short of that would have worked. They killed a god and paid the ultimate price for it."

"Like fuck did they!" Lysander snaps, grabbing Kian's shirt. "Please, you're my brother. I can't fix the court like you told me to without you! You can't fucking die! You can't die!" Thunder backs his shout, but Kian doesn't move. Arden kneels next to Arty, closing her eyes and folding her hands across her stomach. He makes sure not to move Arty too far from Kian, so their bodies are still touching. It's how it should be. I can't believe they are gone. My hands tighten on Emrys.

I tear my eyes away from Emrys to Lysander. "Lysander, please look at me."

Lysander is beyond reason. Terrin and Grayson stand by me, and they are silent. I know what they are going to say, and I won't hear it. I can't hear them say Emrys is gone.

"None of them are breathing, Elle." Terrin kneels next to me. "I'm sorry—"

"NO!" I roar, gripping Emrys to me, my heart breaking even if I won't accept it. "Lysander, please. I need you to check Emrys."

Lysander is frozen, staring at his brother, desperately trying to heal him, with tears flowing down his face. I don't know whose emotions belong to whom. It's all the same. The same screaming grief and heartbreak. "He's my brother."

"I know." My voice breaks. "And he's gone. Arty is gone." I can barely look at her without feeling my heart snapping in two. She came to save me one more time, and she died for me. For us. "But Emrys, Emrys, please."

He gives me a shaky nod. Lysander barely manages to crawl past Kian's body to put his hand on Emrys, right over mine. The water flows around Emrys's body, but it doesn't glow. Nothing happens. Thunder cracks across the sky as Lysander lifts his eyes to mine. "He's gone."

No. "NO!" I scream at them all, pulling Emrys with me. I press my forehead against his, sobbing as I clutch his top. "Emrys, please. Please."

I hear him, just in my mind, just for a moment. "Find me in the Mist. Share a boat with me."

The boats. The Mist. Grayson's Court...he's where the dead go. It's a chance, and the dreams...it was Emrys showing me where he was waiting for me. He never left. The dreams were never just dreams, and I knew it. He came to see me, but he also came to show me how to save him in the end. I don't know how he managed it, but I am never giving up on any of my mates, and I will risk dying on a dream of saving him. I stand up, wiping water and strands of my wet hair from my face. "I have to go. I have to go and take him with me. I need you to trust me. I have to go. Just please look after each other until we are back."

"I'll come with you," Terrin offers.

Grayson meets my eyes. "Elle, where are you going? Why—"

"I don't have time to explain it all," I answer them as I make a portal to Grayson's court. Using the air, using Emrys's powers, I lift him into the air. "Please, just trust me."

"We do. If you have to do this, then we will wait for you," Arden softly replies.

"You can't go into the Mist. Only death walks there…" Grayson warns.

I lift my head high. "My court controls death. I am the queen of the Spirit Court, and I have used my power to slow his last moments down. There is no place death cannot walk and therefore, nothing can stop me from going in there and taking my mate's soul back. He is waiting for me. Death will fucking bow, because I am done losing him." I walk straight through to the other side of the portal, onto the grassy green mountains where the death mist floats in the air. There is a smell in the air that borders on sweet and as cruel as death, all at the same time.

I walk through the grass to the edge of the Mist, standing before the fog and staring into it. It's wrapped around the edge of the Earth Court, and I came here once with Grayson to send his mother into the Mist. The dragons send all of their dead here, but I don't know if a living person has ever made the trip over, and I doubt it. I have to believe I'm not wrong. I have to believe Emrys is waiting for me. I'd wait for him. I'd wait for them all.

There is a single boat lined up at the edge of the Mist, the shimmering veil of it just behind. Gently, I lay Emrys in the boat before climbing in with him. I use the air gift to blow the boat forward, right into the Mist. This is madness, I know it, but I look down at Emrys as we float forward into somewhere that only death will judge us. I run my fingers down his cheek. "Please be there. I'm not leaving without you." I lean down and kiss his forehead. "You can't leave me, not now, not ever." My tears fall from my face onto his as the Mist covers us. It parts slowly and my magic stops working, the boat pausing in a clearing in the deep mist, like fog I can't see through.

I look into it, feeling like someone or something is watching me. "Please give him back. If he dies, then it was for nothing. Arty and Kian are dead for nothing. All this didn't save him anyway. He can't die." I rest my head on his chest, wishing I could feel and hear his heart beat. "EMRYS!" I scream into the darkness, and nothing echoes back. I can't see anything in it, just a fog that endlessly spreads in every direction. I stand up, tightening my hands into fists. He doesn't deserve this. I am the spirit queen. I am the queen of death. I can save him!

"If you're going to take anyone's life, then take mine, because he never, ever deserved this! He is good, he is pure, he killed Ares to save this world, and now his life has been taken. If there is any good, anything pure left here, please, please give him back to me. I love him. I love him so much and I want him back. I'm not leaving without him. Fuck the rest of the world if I can't have him!"

Massive dragons appear in the darkness of the fog, and they look like they're made maybe of stone, and the Mist has bent to smother their bodies in a sparkling haze. They lean down, stretching their wings out, their eyes sparkling like a thousand colours. One is clearly male and the other female. A couple. They talk, not out loud, but straight into my mind. "No one comes to the place of the dead and demands a life."

I lift my chin. "I do," I snarl, getting angry. "I come here because I am queen of this place. Because I will spend the rest of my life making sure this world thrives. I deserve to have him at my side, and we can rule together. He deserves to live. So please, I am begging whoever you are to give him back. I know he is here, waiting for me. He waited."

"We are the Dragon Gods, known in this world. In others, we are known as Darkness and Light, as the Moon Goddess and the God of Hell. We collect souls from all worlds and, yes, he is here." My heart races. "We have watched you. You are a goddess in your own right, and you have fixed this world. You have never stopped and fought endlessly. For that reason and only this once, we will allow the dead to walk back."

"My life for his?"

"No, your servitude in this world in exchange for the return of his soul," they command together.

"It's a deal." I look down as Emrys blinks,

gasping for air, and he wakes. He's alive. I throw myself on him and he grunts as he catches me, laughing as he holds me tight to his chest. The dragons fly away, sending our boat flying straight out of the Mist. By some miracle, I saved him, and I'm never letting him go again.

CHAPTER 15

This evening, I do what I do every time I wake up from a bad nightmare, and I look for my mates to check they are alive. Emrys is sleeping next to me, finally with some colour back in his cheeks after two weeks of constant healers. I might have brought him back from the dead, which has somehow become a legend around Ayiolyn, but Ares wrecked his body in the meantime. Grayson is on my other side, his arm thrown over his face and his other arm resting across my stomach. I ease it to the side and sit up, wrapping my arms around my knees. Arden is on the sofa, stretched out, and Lysander is on a makeshift pull-out bed by the bathroom. Terrin still hasn't gotten used to his human form, and he is sleeping in dragon form on the wrap-around balcony.

Only in the middle of the night do I get a moment to remember that Arty and Kian are gone. Telling everyone about their deaths when we got back was heartbreaking, and bringing their bodies here was just as bad. Even Hope cried, and we all bowed to them, because we owe them everything. I wish I knew if they are happy now and if they are still together in wherever death took them next. I want to tell Arty so much, tell her I love her and thank her. I want to thank them both.

Lysander and his mother have grown closer in their mourning, and the entire Water Court has thrown an endless funeral leading up to tomorrow. The funeral arrangements are tomorrow, to send their bodies into the Mist, and they can be at peace. There are so many bodies, so many funerals from the Air Court to go into the Mist that I know funerals are going to last for months.

Everything is so quiet in the night, and I close my eyes, remembering that I'm safe. My mates are safe. I don't think there will ever be a point I won't remember my mate dying in my arms, not just once, but twice, and how I very nearly lost him for good. A rustle from the balcony makes my gaze shoot over, and I see the outline of a figure. I can see Terrin's dragon stretched out on the other side, so it isn't him.

I quietly climb out of the bed, not wanting to wake anyone. Everything is such a mess, and we are all working from the moment we get up till the moment we get back to our room for dinner and bed. I know it won't always be like this, but getting order in the courts is important. Making sure everyone has food and housing is important. Our people are important, and we can suffer for a while.

I find my uncle standing outside. "What are you doing here?" I whisper, shutting the door behind me. I glance at Terrin, but he is a heavy sleeper and completely out of it. "I thought you'd gone back to Earth."

"I had until an old friend asked me to come back just this once. I have some good news to share with you first." His gaze sends fear lacing across my chest, even when I know he wouldn't hurt me. It's a normal response to the god of nightmares. "I am to have a child next year."

I smile. "Congratulations."

237

"Tell me you'll bring your own children to meet ours one day on Earth," he demands. "I don't want you to never come to Earth and see us."

"Aww, you saying you love me?" I tease him, and he rolls his eyes. "You could stay here in Ayiolyn. I'd like that."

He huffs like an old man. I suppose he is one, being an ancient god, but he looks like a late-twenties supermodel with crazy dark vibes. "My home is on Earth with my mate. Humans are so easily scared. There's nowhere else I'd prefer to be."

A laugh escapes me, knowing he's deadly serious about frightening humans for the rest of his life. Phobos literally has a Halloween-based island that runs all year round. He somehow lured his mate there, from the stories he told us before he left. He opens a portal, one on the ground, and it's weird. "It's a gift."

I peer into it. "I'm confused. What is a gift? Where does that lead?"

"It's a doorway to hell." He grins like that's a present.

"You want me to go to hell? Well, Uncle, it's lovely to see you too, but…" I grin.

"Snarky sarcasm suits you. I'd be annoyed if I hadn't taught you that myself. Now come on." He walks into the portal and down the steps. Reluctantly, I follow him, trusting my uncle. The steps go on and on, and my legs hurt by the time we come down what must be a thousand steps into a place that's actually very beautiful. If this is hell, then God knows what heaven must look like.

A big ancient house takes up the centre of the huge cavern, and purple fires burst up into the air all the way around it. Everything glows a deep purple, and it's so bright it hurts to stare for too long. The house itself is green though, the darkest shade, with exotic plants and trees all the way around it. Phobos doesn't lead me to the house, but around it to the back, along a stone path to where a massive garden stretches for miles below with a small lake in the centre. The purple light reflects off the black shiny stone above, and I look down at the natural pool, which is red and black instead of blue. It glitters like someone threw a dozen buckets of glitter into the water.

It's not empty.

Arty and Kian are in the water, and they're

laughing, splashing each other. Just having fun like they didn't die to save the world. I take a step forward, but Phobos grabs my arm to stop me. "You can't communicate with the dead. It would confuse them and cause them pain. Their life is over, and their afterlife is to be shared only with the souls they love. Hades and Persephone wanted you to see this so you can tell Lysander he is well, because you were her sister in every right known to the gods."

Arty. Her hair is wavy and wet, and she looks so carefree. So, so happy. Tears fall down my chin, dripping onto my hands. "You could have brought Lysander here to see for himself with me."

"The water king cannot come. The invite was only for you, as this takes great magic," Phobos softly explains. "There are not many alive who get a glimpse of death and live to tell the tale."

"Thank you," I whisper to the gods that rule hell. I watch my friends for a long while, knowing this is the last time. For a second, I see the moment I met Arty in a room in the castle and how joyful she was, how alive she was. I remember her like that, remember her light and how that light eventually led to her saving the world. Because she did. She saved them all, even if most of the world won't remember that in the generations to come. I am going to tell my children about her and Kian and how they loved each other so much.

"They are honoured guests. Making such a sacrifice of their lives means that they will live like royalty. Their souls remain forever here. So will you, when it is your time," Phobos explains to me. "They will never feel pain, never want for anything ever again. True peace in death."

There is nothing I could have wanted more for them. "I feel guilty that I get to live, and they don't."

Phobos wraps his arm around my shoulders. "Only natural. I sensed your guilt and struggle. I asked for this." He kisses the top of my head. "You were my practice child, and I'm proud of you."

"Practice child? Please don't tell me you're going to train your own kid like me?" I shove him away, and he roars with laughter. I smile at him when he winks. "Aphrodite and Ares, where are they?"

His eyes drift over and look out in the far

distance. I follow his line of sight to where there is a pit. A black pit with strange red creatures that almost look like three-headed dogs that guard all the surrounding way in a circle. Inside that darkness, something awful sends shivers down my spine. "They are burning in hell forever, and they will never leave."

I don't spend too much time dwelling on that as I look back, it's enough to know they are dead and suffering for their actions. Tears keep falling down my cheeks, and Phobos leans over, wiping one away. "Come on, niece. Death is not always ugly. It can be beautiful. That girl down there, all she ever wanted to do was to have someone that's worth dying for. She found you. She found him." He smiles softly. "Kian wanted to find someone to fall in love with, and to give his brother a reason to make everything better in the court he grew up in. He did both. Lysander will change the court forever for his brother, and never again will the Water Court know brutality. This is a happy ending, even with death. Death can be stunning."

Arty looks up and I feel like she can actually see me. She smiles so widely, only for a second, and then she turns back to Kian, kissing him softly. "Goodbye, Arty." I hope my whisper carries to her, to her soul, because one day, I will find her again. "It's time to go," I whisper, my voice broken with emotion. When I get back, I go straight through the doors and go to Lysander. His eyes widen as he wakes up. He smiles at me, although groggily, and wraps his arms around my waist. There's so much sadness in his eyes that never goes away. I curl up onto his lap. "I just saw your brother. He was swimming with Arty in a lake in hell. They're happy."

"What are you talking about, spirit witch?" he groans into my neck.

I lean into my mate and sigh. "Just that everything is over, and the ghosts are happy."

"*E*lle, do you want a lemonade or a Coke?"

Arden's shout echoes across the deck, and I lean back, smiling at him. He is tanned from the sun and shirtless to show it off. "Coke, please!"

He heads inside to the cooler, and Lysander catches my gaze as my purple hair blows across my face. I tuck it away, seeing a few dark strands coming through. "I will never understand your excitement when Phobos and his family come with those as gifts."

"Hey, if you didn't grow up in the human world, you wouldn't get it," I mutter before sticking my tongue out at him. His eyes darken and he nearly gets hit in the head by a flying ball thrown by Terrin. The two of them are terrors when they play ball, and the one time I took them to a football match on Earth flashes into my mind. They completely forgot the other players were human, and the match was for charity. They destroyed the pitch and set it on fire. By accident, according to them both. Terrin laughs as Lysander glowers at him. "Fucking cheater."

"Don't be distracted, then, dickhead." He taunts Lysander like it's a sport. The two of them have become best friends over the years, and it was an unexpected friendship. Terrin helped me guide Lysander through his grief, and on the darkest days, we just stayed together. There is something perfect about just staying together when you don't want anything more than that.

The chimes echo in my ears as I turn back to the water and continue watching it, my feet in the cold seawater of the Air Court. A massive statue was constructed by Emrys two years ago, and it's beautiful. It makes a constant noise. Thousands of little chimes are attached all the way around a stone tornado, spinning up into the sky. Every chime is for a family that was lost, a name written on the chimes to echo forever. They were handmade by the survivors of the Air Court and placed here for everyone to come and see.

I watch it from our royal floating house, right on the lake itself. It's our favourite place to come, especially this time of year, around the time that the Air Court fell five years ago. It's a hard time for Emrys, especially considering he lost everything this day, and it was something he was forced to watch through Ares's hold on his body. This place belonged to his family and now to him, and we all love it here. We have a home in every court, something public and something private. Emrys's mum was lovely enough to stock it with food and drinks for us, like she does every year.

This is our only home in the Air Court. The floating castle was destroyed by Ares's death, and none of us wanted to go back to the ruins, especially not Emrys. He is haunted even now by the memories that come back to him, but on those days, I stay at his side from dawn to dusk. Thankfully, there were more survivors than we knew about. People hid and waited for Emrys to come for them.

"Here you go," Arden hands me a Coke in a tall blue glass with a tiny lemon and lots of ice, just how I like it. "Sure you don't want any wine? I brought your favourite here."

"It's a bit early for wine," I lie. I always want wine, but I won't be having it for a long time. Arden kisses the top of my head as Emrys calls him back to the BBQ, where he and Grayson are bickering over how to spice the food. Laughter carries to my ears from across the lake, and I look over at the other houses and the children running across the deck. The Air Court population is coming back. Slowly but surely. It reminds me of the Spirit Court, which my mother tells me every day that it is getting back to how it was before the court fell. But better. Bigger. Peace was always the goal and, oddly enough, I know we have it.

Terrin kept the crown of the West long after the battle was won. We are finally united with them, something no ruler of Ayiolyn has ever been able to do. We have regular trade routes set up and even a dragon rider academy in the West for anyone who wants to train a wild dragon and join the army. Many of our people who don't have magic go across the borders to train there and with our blessing. We have a peace agreement in place that will last indefinitely.

Overall, I did everything that I promised, and I hope that our actions last for the generations to come after us. I hope Arty and Kian are proud of us. There's not a day that goes by that I don't think of them though and the loss we took. The warm breeze blows across my body as the sun shines down, and I smile at the sky. I know they are happy, and I remind myself of that.

"Did you see Hope's kid climbing the wall yesterday?" Arden asks Grayson. "He is so fast, and Hope looked mighty pissed off. Livia had to grab him and bring him down. Again."

I grin to myself. Hope's son, Laurent, is a rascal and breaks every rule he possibly can. I love him. He lives in the Water Court with his parents, but they regularly bring the three-year-old over to mess up our castle as well as our place and test the patience of the castle's never-ending snack deliveries. I don't think I've ever seen so many different types and flavours of cake.

I glance over my shoulder at my mates. Lysander is grinning. He loves this place. Even if he moves the house near the waterfall every night and pretends he didn't do anything, just to piss off Emrys. Arden, who is not a huge fan of a floating house on water, still smiles every time we agree to come here for a few weeks to be alone. We are working in his court for a spell breaker for his grandfather, and I know we are close. It doesn't matter how many years it takes; we won't forget him. Emrys loves being in his court, and Grayson comes here more than us now. His sister has married an Air Court guard who survived the gods, and they bonded over the recovery of the courts. He is a good kid, and he is terrified of Grayson. I regularly remind him Gray is all bark and no bite. I especially reminded Gray how much his sister loved her boyfriend when he came to ask Gray if he could ask her to marry him last year. They got married a month ago, and they are currently travelling around the courts on a honeymoon.

My grandmother and Cronus love this court too, and they made their home on one of the islands, which is mostly forest. They claimed it for themselves as a reward for helping in the war, and none of us really wanted to disagree. Especially when they took their dead army there, which all of us were very glad about, as the rotting bodies really smell after a while. We wouldn't have won the battle at the Spirit Court without them, and I get to see my grandmother regularly. It is nice when we come here though; it's just us, without the pressure of all the courts, the pressure of everything that we end up having to do when we go into any of the big castles despite having very good ruling councils we leave behind. Livia is the leader of mine, and she chose everyone in it, along with my mother.

I stand up and raise my arms above my head after putting my Coke down. I'm dressed in the sluttiest bikini I found on a trip to Earth last year with Hope and Livia. They all look, and the heat of their gaze makes my skin pebble everywhere. Tonight is going to be fun. Five years together, and every single time they touch me, nothing has changed. The same fire, the same burn, and the need for more. It's endless. I pull my cover-up on, throwing it over my shoulders. "Can we talk?"

They go silent and watch me, all of them frowning at my tone. "Everything alright?"

I never quite get used to all of their attention at once, and it makes me want to stutter over my words. I mean, there have been several drunk nights where I've had all of their attention at once in a naked way, and I struggled to walk the next day, but it was amazing. At this time, though, I'm more nervous. I've been using my magic to hide the extra scent wrapped around me until we got here and were alone. I found out three days ago, and it worked out well that all of them have been so busy with royal duties. I push the magic away, stopping it from protecting what I've been keeping hidden. It takes them a second. Lysander's eyes widen first, a look of shock that leaves him silent. That's a first. Emrys walks over and kneels in front of me, resting his head on my stomach. I feel him shaking slightly.

Arden has tears in his eyes, but he is shocked too, and it's Grayson who speaks first, awe marking his words. "Are you pregnant?"

"Are there babies in there? As in more than one?" Terrin whispers as Emrys kisses my stomach. I run my hands through his hair. "Yes. Two. Twins."

"The babies smell like all of us," Lysander whispers, but there is love in his voice. Like he loves them already, like I do. I might not know their names, what they sound like or what their favourite thing is, but I know I'd do anything to find out. To be there for their first steps, first laugh and every first. It makes everything worth all the fighting we've been through. "How?"

"Magic." I wipe my cheeks. "Somehow, someway, these babies are a part of all of us, and they are our future."

"You're going to be the best mother." Grayson comes closer and kisses my cheek. They crowd around me, my mates, the fathers of my children, and my kings.

We are a court of dragons at peace, and it wasn't something I ever thought would happen. Could happen even. The rest of the day, we spend on the deck, eating and talking about our future children, and I spend all of it imagining what my boys are going to be like. What they will sound like when they laugh or what will be their favourite toy.

I can't wait to tell my mum and grandmother if they don't know already. The pair of them were asking strange questions about timing and life a week ago when we met up, and I thought it was odd. The pair of them always seem to know everything beforehand, but I expect they will be delighted. I never told them about the twins and how I knew about them. That knowledge was personal between my mates and me. And the matron, but none of us have seen her since I went into the darkness, which is now gone. The space it was is just a room now, but the castle is still very much alive somehow. We all speculate that the castle itself is now what is left of the darkness and Matron. But who knows?

"Are you sure you're not tired?" Arden questions, leaning on the door to our massive bedroom. The bed is enormous enough for all six of us to easily sleep in it, with cream bedding, big pillows, and cushions that Emrys picked out. We often don't all share the same room, as we all like our own space now and again. Terrin walks in behind Arden, patting his arm. "I was just checking on our mate to see if she is tired or not."

"I'm pregnant, not sick," I pout, watching Arden. "Close the door?"

He shuts it without even blinking. Terrin pulls his shirt off at the same time, and both of them descend on me. Arden and Terrin together? It's one of my favourite times. Lysander likes me alone. Emrys and Grayson sometimes prefer me together, but Arden and Terrin? This is normal for us, and I love it. I love every second of their attention. Terrin reaches me first and shadows. His magic, which he has a good control over now, makes my bikini completely disappear.

I gasp as he picks me up and lays me gently on the bed, climbing over me to kiss me. The moment his lips find mine, heat explodes through my body and burns up my spine. Terrin kisses down my neck, then my chest before kneeling between my legs and parting me. Terrin looks at me like I'm his own personal goddess, and Arden groans. "Fuck, I'll never get bored of seeing your pussy."

I don't get a second to reply to Arden, who has lost his clothes and is climbing onto the bed. Terrin flips me over, pulling me up on my knees and immediately sinking his tongue right onto my clit. Careful, trained strokes of his tongue have me panting and building to an orgasm in seconds, and I know he won't stop, not until I've finished at least two times. Arden usually likes to make me beg first.

I moan as Arden kneels in front of me, grabbing my chin, and I lean forward to take his hard cock into my mouth. His hand tightens on my chin, his other hand finding my hair and guiding my movements to how he likes it. I can barely focus on Arden when Terrin sends me crashing into an orgasm, his masculine laugh echoing through our bond in my mind. "More, mate?" I love when he uses our bond to sense what I want, how I want everything. I know Arden does the same, and I love to peek into his mind to know what he wants right now, how he is feeling. The mate bond is truly an honour to have, and I never want to lose our connection.

"Always," I moan back to him in my mind, even when I know we want the same thing. More of this. More of us. Us, never ending. I hear him scuffling, moving until the tip of his hard cock presses against my opening, pushing before he completely sinks into me with a groan. His pleasure blasts down the bond in a wave, mixing with Arden's pleasure and mine. Terrin holds my hips as he slams into me, and Arden groans in a way I know he is close. I suck on his cock a little more, and he groans, taking his cock out to come across my tits. Another orgasm slams down my spine, and Terrin stills with me, filling me with his own finish. We all fall back on the bed, and I nestle in the middle of them. Their warm bodies are perfect to lie between. Terrin kisses my forehead. "I love you."

Arden's arm rests across my stomach, his fingers tracing my belly as I use my water powers to wash everything off us and air to dry us and move a blanket across the room, laying it over us both. Arden keeps his hand on my stomach the entire time, and I look up at my fire king. "They will be kings of the courts."

I imagine that future, our children ruling in peace, and I realise it's all we ever wanted.

BONUS HALLOWEEN EPILOGUE

Join my newsletter below to receive a free bonus special Halloween Epilogue set ten years in the future and meet the twins—Link here.

AFTERWORD

This book, like all my others, is for my family
and for my readers.

Thank you.

Want to learn about Phobos and his mate? This
short Halloween novella is their story and based
in this world.

Court of Dragons and Pumpkins.

ABOUT G. BAILEY

G. Bailey is a USA Today and international bestselling author of books that are filled with everything from dragons to pirates. Plus, fantasy worlds and breath-taking adventures.
G. Bailey is from England and loves rainy days with her family.

(You can find exclusive teasers, random giveaways, and sneak peeks of new books on the way in Bailey's Pack on Facebook or on TikTok— gbaileybooks)
FIND MORE BOOKS BY G. BAILEY ON AMAZON...
LINK HERE.

MORE BOOKS BY G. BAILEY

HER GUARDIANS SERIES

HER FATE SERIES

PROTECTED BY DRAGONS SERIES

LOST TIME ACADEMY SERIES

THE DEMON ACADEMY SERIES

DARK ANGEL ACADEMY SERIES

SHADOWBORN ACADEMY SERIES

DARK FAE PARANORMAL PRISON SERIES

SAVED BY PIRATES SERIES

THE MARKED SERIES

HOLLY OAK ACADEMY SERIES

THE ALPHA BROTHERS SERIES

A DEMON'S FALL SERIES

THE FAMILIAR EMPIRE SERIES

FROM THE STARS SERIES

THE FOREST PACK SERIES

THE SECRET GODS PRISON SERIES

THE REJECTED MATE SERIES

FALL MOUNTAIN SHIFTERS SERIES

ROYAL REAPERS ACADEMY SERIES

THE EVERLASTING CURSE SERIES

THE MOON ALPHA SERIES

THE DRAGON CROWN SERIES

CHRYSALIS PACK SERIES

THE NEXUS SERIES

DESCRIPTION OF BONUS READ.

Dragons don't exist anymore. Neither do their legendary fae riders…until I stumble into a mansion full of them.

It turns out the last of the dragon rider fae have been locked in a trap, a mansion with no doors, no way to leave for five hundred years, and I'm the first fae to enter. The dragon fae riders know nothing of the world outside or the vampyres who have taken over in their absence, and most don't trust me.

Especially not Ziven—king of the forgotten Moon Dynasty.

The gorgeous but cruel king demands I enter the Decidere, a ritual for all fae over the age of twenty. It's a deadly trial in the dragons' caves below the mansion, and if you're weak, you're dead. Ziven marks me as a traitor, and he doesn't believe anything I say. He wants me to lose. The Sun Dynasty king takes me in, helps me and is kind. With his help, I might last a week.

With Ziven doing everything he can to end me, my ability to escape the mansion seeming impossible, and dragons literally burning the ground at my feet, I don't know how I'm going to live through this.

You need to be brave. You need to be a warrior…or the dragons will know.

My name is Story Dehana, and I escaped the vampyres, only to find myself trapped once again with a new enemy who might be worse.

A *Vow of Dragons and Storms* is the first book in The Lost Fae Riders Series. This is a full-

length fantasy, dragon-rider romance with an enemy who might become a lover, found family, the best romance tropes, and a main character who loves reading almost as much as you.

A VOW OF DRAGONS AND STORMS

Page One.
To my reader—
I was a dragon rider, and if
you're reading this, I must be
dead.

When a female seeks revenge, society often labels her a monster. I'm the monster in the vampyre society, but they won't cage me ever again.

The wind and rain whips through my red and black locks of hair as I run, strands lashing my bruised cheek and cut lip every so often. They are nothing compared to the burning of my broken ribs from the rock I just fell over, but I use the pain to fuel myself. The damp moss on the surrounding trees is all I can smell as I run, my legs aching with every slam of my bare feet on the forest floor.

Keep running.

Don't let them catch you.

You are never going to be a slave to them again, Story Dehana.

Tears fill my eyes as it feels like he is right at my side, whispering encouragement in my ear. My best friend who always believed in me...but he is gone now, and if they catch me, he died for *nothing*. Narrowly missing a tree, I turn to the left and stumble onto an old stone path, parts of which look like they have been well hidden under years' worth of plants and dead leaves. In uncovered parts, the soggy mud between the massive stones threatens to pull me in, but I can't stop. I won't.

An unnatural silence fills the air, and my heart races.

The vampyres have found me.

I stop, spinning around, breathing heavily as sweat drips down my neck. I have to hide until they pass. I pray to the deities for a safe haven, even if they have shunned me for as long as I can remember. My eyes frantically search for somewhere to hide, somewhere they wouldn't sense me. My heart leaps with hope when the moonlight shines down through the thick green trees, illuminating the spiralling towers of some kind of house.

If the house has thick enough walls, they might not be able to hear my heartbeat. If I could find a basement... I smile for the first time since entering this forest. Running here was never the plan, but it all went wrong. I might be able to hide from them in there, at least long enough for the vampyres to pass through this part of the Hydra Forest. I blow out one shaky breath before leaving the stone path and running straight towards the spiralling towers that climb higher than the trees themselves. That's saying something, as the trees around here are gigantic, taller than any building I've ever seen, taller than the vampyres' mighty castles.

Nearly tripping over several logs, I focus on the ground as I run until the forest floor changes to a marked stone pathway. The path leads up to massive metal gates, which are swung open, held in place by thick ivy that has grown over the gates and broken them in parts. At the bottom of the path is a mansion, sitting in the forest, like the deities themselves dropped it here for me. It's old, mostly derelict, and I bet it's close to falling down. Four towers mark the corners, with a triangular pointed roof in the middle. A colossal round stained glass window is in the middle of the building, but it's too dusty and covered in dirt for me to see what is pictured. There are hundreds of triangle windows around the dark stone building, and its massive front doors look slightly ajar. There's no light coming from inside, just pitch darkness from what I can see. It's creepy, but I don't have a choice.

I don't know what this mansion is doing out here; I wasn't even aware there were buildings inside the Hydra Forest, and I would know, as I've looked over the maps in the weapons room a hundred times. It's meant to be empty, abandoned to the world. But right now, that mansion is going to be my salvation.

The unnerving silence fills the cold air, like a mist crawling through the forest floor that promises death. A silence that's only brought by the vampyres when they're hunting their prey. I need to move. If the birds, rabbits, foxes, and all creatures go silent, then death is not too far away. Death would be a mercy for what I will get if they manage to capture me. I sprint as fast as I possibly can down the path, which is remarkably solid considering that this place must be hundreds of years old. It doesn't look like a single soul has walked here in a long time.

Daring to glance behind me, I'm surprised to see the gates have slammed shut, locking me into this gigantic garden of the mansion. I frown at that for a second, but I don't have time to dwell on it, to think about how the gates even shut themselves, when I hear branches cracking in the forest. They are getting close. It's seconds before I'm standing in front of the massive oak doors that lead into the mansion. They're slightly open, a small enough gap for me to slide through, and I don't wait. With my heart racing, I grab the wood door and slowly inch myself through the gap, pushing with all my strength to get through. With a final tug, I fall out of the gap, inside the mansion, right onto hard, cold stone floors and my ribs scream in pain. The doors slam shut behind me, the bang echoing loudly.

My eyes shoot up as lights burn to life on the ceiling, magic held within crystals that form a chandelier that is bigger than me. The square room has beautiful mosaic walls, grey stone floors, and there are two other doors, both the same oak as the front.

This mansion is not derelict inside...and I don't think I'm alone. A statue of some kind sits between the doors on the other side, and it's a creature on all fours. It has massive wings spread out and a fierce mouth, baring rows of teeth. It's familiar...I just can't remember the name of the creature for a moment until it hits me. Dragon. An extinct creature from the old times. I saw a painting of one in the forbidden books my tutor gave me, only briefly, and it stuck with me how terrifying they look. The dragons and their dragon fae riders are nothing but a whispered fairy tale that the lessborn fae tell their children so they don't run away into the forests.

How is that statue possible? Not only are dragons extinct, any mention of them is a death sentence. I crawl backwards until my back hits the door. I need to get out of here. I reach up, looking for a handle, finding none. I'm patting the door for some kind of way to get out when I hear a footstep behind me. I turn back to see a man standing in front of the statue, like he appeared out of thin air. The doors never made a sound. The stone wings of the statue spread out behind the stranger, making them almost look like they're his wings, like this beautiful man could take off into the skies. He looks surprised, absolutely shocked. That makes two of us.

He watches me with pure astonishment for a long time until it's just uncomfortable. Am I safer in here with this stranger or in the forest with the vampyres hunting me?

"Who are you?" His voice is thick, deeper and stranger than any accent I've ever heard before.

"I could say the same thing." My voice is breathless as I ascend to my feet, plastering my back to the door. "I think I've walked into the wrong place. I should get going now, but I can't find a handle. How do you open the door?"

The male's eyes widen a fraction. "You're not going anywhere. No one just walks into here. The dynasty royals will decide what to do with you."

"Royals?" I dare to ask, my skin paling. There can't be vampyre royals here. There can't. I've just escaped them. What if I ran into one of their traps? Why would they be out here in the forest in the middle of nowhere without guards? I can't breathe, I can't move, as the male walks to me. He doesn't move like any vampyre I've seen or look like them either. His skin is too warm, his hair too blond, too perfect. I do the best thing that I possibly can think of, I dart around him and run, heading straight towards the other doors. I barely get two steps before he's roughly grabbed me from behind. Something hard slams into the back of my head just as my fingers graze the wing of the dragon.

A VOW OF DRAGONS AND STORMS

Page Two.

Dragons are beautiful creatures that should be feared by everyone but the one fae they choose as their rider. I fought the stones for my dragon, and if you keep reading, maybe you will be one too.

"Don't worry. They'll just do a test and then we'll find out where you go. Okay?"

My mother's soft words do little to settle the nerves in the pit of my stomach, no matter how *many times she repeats herself. Maybe she has convinced her own heart to stop beating as fast as mine. Her long red hair is braided down her back, like mine, but she doesn't have the black-ness that crawls up my locks and makes people stare. Will my hair make me stand out today? Will how pale and curvy I am? Will the fact I have tipped fae ears, even when most don't anymore? My insecurities are like a never-ending song in my mind, repeating over and over, until I've forgotten the point of the sweet song that I had begun listening to. Until my thoughts are as real to me as the vibrant silver moon in the night sky each night.*

I play with the end of my braid as we stand before the thin black doors that lead into the basement of the processing district. My mother kisses the top of my head. "Happy birth year, darling girl. I don't think I got a moment to say that." Happy birth year *seems inappropriate, considering no part of today will be happy.*

I'm fourteen this birth year, and for fae, it's a cursed year. On every fae's fourteenth birth year, you're officially classed as an adult. At least the lessborn fae like me are. There are three places the lessborn fae are divided into, depending on the results of today's test. The breeders—like where I live with my mother. I wince at the idea of returning there. My mum is classed as an unsuccessful breeder, being she only ever had me and no other children, despite many suitors. Every other family I know has five or six children, some as many as nine, and that is normal for female fae breeders. We were always outcasts because it's just me and her, but I like that. I like that I get her attention all of the time. But it doesn't mean I want to be there. What if I'm unsuccessful as a breeder? I don't think I even want children, though I'm not sure it's an option for me to want things, but being a breeder is the best option.

The second is a worker, sent to the mines to collect gold, silver or crystals for the vampyres until my back breaks or a rock crushes me. The third option...my mother won't even speak about the third option, but I've heard it from the fae I grew up around. They whisper it around—the blood slaves. The blood slaves are rejects of society, the ones that don't fit in with the workers in the mines because their bodies aren't able or they're not successfully able to be a breeder. Today's check decides everything.

"Story Dehana, come forward." I lift my hand, like she doesn't know exactly who I am. There are four families here. The rest of the people my age are boys. The fae female waves her hand at us, her eyes drifting to my mother for a second, and she blinks in surprise. She is powerborn, like I'm told my father was before he died. The markings on her cheek tell me she is a healer, a flower wrapped around a star, and they match the many markings of power on her hands—all flowers, different ones, that move against her skin like they are alive. The power-born fae get a choice in their careers, in their lives, but they rule nothing like the rest of us. Fae are slaves to the vampyres, no matter what you're born as. "Come in, come in."

My mother all but tugs me forward with her hand, leading me into the cold room. There's a metal bed in the middle, with a single white cushion, and the walls are blank. The woman shuts the door behind me. "Go lie down, Story. I will be right with you." Her voice is quiet as she addresses my mother. "It's good to see you, Ylene. You haven't aged a day."

"You're too kind, Blaire. How is your son?" my mother whispers back.

She touches her neck where another marking is. This one is a diamond, which marks the birth of a child. "Growing up fast. Too fast."

My mother looks at me, light shining in her dark forest green eyes that are exactly the same as mine. "I know the feeling, my old friend." She blinks a few times, straightening her back and smiling like she hasn't got a worry in the world. "Shall we?"

Blaire faces me and rubs her hands together as she closes the space between us. "I only need to take a drop of your blood, and then I'll be able to see where you're suitable for. Your blood holds all the answers of your body to me, and it will show me what your fate shall be."

"Okay." My voice shakes. I'm not brave, not like my mother. I'm not a warrior like my father was.

"This will all be over soon," Blaire gently tells me, tucking away her loose strands of brown hair. I'm not sure how my mother knows this powerborn fae, but I don't have time to question her. I sit down as Blaire comes over, a small needle and a glass tube in her hands. She

pricks my finger, and I barely feel the pain before a small amount of my red blood trickles into the tube.

I can practically hear my heart racing in my ear, like a constant drum, as I stare at Blaire's back. Bright orange magic, a rare magic for powerborn fae, flashes in front of her, and she goes still. She seems to do it two—no, three— times before she looks over her shoulder. I've always been good at reading people's eyes, and her blue eyes are screaming a thousand words, and none of them good.

She clears her throat. "Ylene, can I speak to you outside?" She points to a door. "Just out there?" Sensing my gaze, Blaire looks at me. "There's nothing to worry about...I just need to speak to your mother for a second." Of course, when adults tell you there's nothing to worry about, there's always something to worry about. I sit up as my mother goes out the side door with her, and they leave it slightly cracked open. I can't help myself as I run over, hiding just behind the door so I can hear them.

"Oh, Ylene, I'm so, so sorry," Blaire is exclaiming.

My mother seems to pause before she asks a

question that determines my entire future with barely a whisper. "What are you sorry about?"

"She's not eligible for the breeders or the workers, and I'm just sorry. So sorry. Story has problems with her ovaries and uterus, a rare condition. We don't even have a name for it, not anymore. I could sense it in her blood," she begins to explain, and my stomach drops. "Her uterus is scarred, her ovaries full of cysts, even now before her monthlies have begun. It must be a birth defect of some kind; the offspring of mixing lessborn and powerborn fae like her... sometimes results in this. She will have difficult monthly cycles, intense, awful pain. She will be weak, and her body will betray her with pain every month and sometimes in between. She will need healers sometimes, and she cannot go to the workers like that. I can't recommend her to either."

I hear my mother move forward. "Yes, she can. Just lie for me, for her father! Please, send her to the breeders. I'll just hide her symptoms. She won't get pregnant, but it happens. It happens all the time. She'll just be kept there. That's how it is." Her voice is spinning into desperation, more panicked, higher pitched by *the second. My heart races as I listen to them deciding my fate.*

"I can't, Ylene. I wish I could. For him,*" she answers, and I believe her, believe the soft tone. She liked my father. "I wish I could, but I cannot. They would just send others to check her, and then they'll find what I did, and she'll still go to the same fate. It would be cruel to attract that much attention her way. They might even kill her for breaking the law. They'd certainly kill both of us."*

"No...NO!" my mother shouts. "You're not sending my daughter to be a blood slave for those—" Her voice skyrockets off the walls.

"Keep it down before someone hears you. The vampyres are always listening around here. I'm so sorry, there isn't another option. I'm going to have to send her to be a blood slave," Blaire firmly states, her voice cracking. "She'll be okay. They're gentle with their blood slaves when they're young. When she gets older, she'll make her own way."

"And I will never see her again. They'll keep her here in this godforsaken city until one vampyre takes it too far and kills her for her blood, like she is nothing more than an animal.

That's all we are to them: lessborn or power-born, we are just blood," my mother hisses with pure venom in her voice. "If her father was alive—"

"Well, he isn't, and neither is my brother. They both died that day! We all live with the consequences of their deaths," Blaire angrily snaps. I wish I knew more about my father, but my mother never speaks much of him. He was a warrior for the fae, and he died fighting for us all. My mother repeats that line anytime I ask her about him. She never tells me anything more, and right now, I wish she'd told me everything she knows so I might be prepared for what is coming.

Silence, thick and empty, echoes between them. Her voice is softer, kind, when she speaks next. "I'll watch out for her myself. I vow it to the deities. I'll make sure she gets a good vampyre master. I'll pick someone to look after her, who won't take it too far. Ever. Not all of them are like the king and royals, Ylene."

My mother's weeping fills the corridor, and I walk away, back to the bed. I lie back on it, looking up at the plain white ceiling, knowing my future is completely and utterly over. I lift my finger, seeing a drop of my blood run down my finger, down my wrist, like it's marking me already. I'm going to be a blood slave, and after today, I'm never going to see my mother again.

The room is spinning when I wake up, and I first see a dome made of pure glass and past that, a million stars burning across the night sky outside. The moon is shining down on me, the silver light so bright. Everything is hazy for a minute as I remember the mansion in the forest, the dragon statue, and the male who hit me over the head when I ran. The room is silent, but I can feel eyes on me. That deep sense that I'm really not alone. Now I've tasted freedom, I'm not sure I ever want to give it up and I think I might like being alone. I don't care what I've walked into here; I'm leaving for the life I want the first chance I get. I lift my head, propping myself up on my elbows, and my mouth drops.

There are at least a thousand pairs of eyes on me, if not more. The glass room is circular, and it's an auditorium, with rows and rows of seats reaching up high. The seats are filled with people, and all of them are silently staring at me. They don't look like vampyres...they are fae. But not like any fae I've seen before. How hard was I hit on the head?

I touch the back of my head, feeling a hard lump and dried blood. "I am awfully sorry my cousin hit you. Please stand up if you can. You are in no danger here." A deep, soft male voice fills the quiet. Following the voice, I look up to see a male sitting on what looks like a throne. It's made of leaves cast in stone, withered and cracked in places but a throne, and on the back is a sun made of gold.

The male on it, he is as pretty as the vampyres, maybe even more. His curly, almost white hair is styled around his handsome features, and his gold eyes are like Nightwell lakes in winter when the rays of the sun light up the surface. His hands are covered in markings. I can't see what they are, but there is a gold sun on his left cheek. He watches me curiously as I stand up, my heart racing fast.

They're all looking at me, and I'm really, really not okay with the attention. I cross my arms tightly and glance around for a way to escape. The long-sleeved black top and the dark leggings that I have on, mostly torn from the forest, make me feel like I'm wearing absolutely nothing in front of them. There are so many of them, whatever these people are. I think they're fae, but they're strange. With all the books I've read, I can't believe I don't know what they are. "I should be leaving. Sorry to have bothered you."

Whispers burst out in the crowds, but the male simply chuckles and grins at me. "If you know how to leave, please do make us aware. We'd very much like to go with you."

I steel my back, looking at the male. "What does that mean? You just walk out."

Now the crowd laughs at me, and my cheeks burn. The male clicks his fingers, and they stop. I'm grateful for that. "I think we probably should start with who we are, and then you can tell us who you are. To start with, my name is King Daegan Caelestis Sunfallen, third of my name, born of the Dynasty of the Sun Dragon. Rider of Odemis. And you are?"

King? There is only one king, a vampyre, and it isn't this guy. I feel like my name is tiny when I say it. "Story Dehana."

"Story," he repeats my name, and he is still smiling. "What do you know of the old times?

Say, your history of what happened five hundred years ago? Tell us a story, *Story*."

I clear my throat, rubbing my arms. Part of me wants to stay silent, but I end up rambling anyway. "History that far back is forbidden to people like me." When his eyebrows rise, I explain, my cheeks brightening. "I'm a lessborn fae, only twenty-two years old, who is—was—a blood slave. History isn't taught to us," I state the facts, and the bitterness leaking from my voice can't be helped. I love to read, but the vampyres lock away their massive libraries from the fae because books are power. Books hold the secrets of the world, the stories of great minds, and they are far more than wood bound together. The books we do have, they tell us nothing interesting but how to stay loyal to the vampyres, how to serve them, how to mine and be a breeder. I had a tutor when I was a child, who snuck me books I should never have had a chance to read. I was lucky, compared to others. That's where I saw the dragon, and I never could forget it. "The old times…do you mean before the vampyres' rule?"

His eyes flare. "Yes, what can you tell us

about the time before the vampyres infested the world?"

Infested? "Not much. There used to be dragons and dragon rider fae according to some, but vampyres claim that they were never real. No one really knows much about it all, and it isn't a topic anyone would dare bring up with a vampyre without fear of losing their head. Why is this important to you?"

He tilts his head to the side, ignoring my question. "Carry on."

I dig my nails into my arm. "I only know that they went missing. Extinct, years ago, but I learnt that from a book I shouldn't have read. It might not be true. They pretty much disappeared overnight, from what the tale said. Vampyres took control and they rule with no competition."

"And the fae? Like you?" he asks. "Are you happy being ruled by vampyres?"

"The fae are obedient to them. That's just how it is." *No, we are not happy.* Happy *is a luxury that no fae is allowed.* It's a cruel, endless world for us. If vampyres didn't like our blood as much as they do, I bet they would have killed us all off a long time ago.

Daegan leans back in his throne. "My father

was one of the five kings of the Dragon Rider Fae Dynasties. The Sun Dragon Dynasty, to be exact."

Blood drains from my face. "Pardon?"

"We never went extinct…we've been here." He spreads his hands out. "Welcome to our endless trap, the mansion that we can never leave. You're the first person that's ever come through the door in five hundred years, and you're going to get us out, fae of our blood. You're going to tell us how you did it."

My heart races as I look around. Five hundred years…and I'm the first one in here? I'm so fucked. "How I got in? I just walked in. I was running—"

"From whom or what?" he interrupts me.

"Vampyres," I whisper. I hate when people interrupt what I'm saying, but I'm too scared to say anything about it. They could kill me for speaking out; my vampyre master would have beaten me for it without a second thought.

"What would they want with you?" he asks, and I gather he doesn't mean it as an insult, just curiosity. I'm a curiosity for all of them. Five hundred years, trapped in this mansion, as the world forgot about them? Kings? Rulers? How is it possible they were just forgotten? They became fairy tales, the people around me here, and dangerous ones at that. If the vampyres knew they were here... No, they can't know. It might actually be safer for me in here, hidden with them, than out there.

I rub my arm. "I was their property. The vampyres." I can't tell them more, about exactly whose property I was, or they'd see me as an enemy. "I don't have magic. I am a lessborn fae, and I haven't got a clue how I walked in."

Daegan picks up a chain hanging around his neck, twisting a sun-shaped amulet hanging from it through his fingers. He looks at a female sitting on a nearby bench. The light-haired woman, thin and beautiful, stands. "Is she telling the truth, Etena?"

"Yes," Etena answers, brushing her long white hair over her shoulder. She walks down the benches and to me, only stopping when we are inches away, and she towers over me. I'm shaking slightly, and I barely notice until she touches my shoulder. Her blue eyes flicker to my hands, like she is looking for something. Eventually she looks up, her eyes running down the braid that pulls my hair from my face, the rest of my messy locks tumbling over my shoulders before she settles on meeting my eyes. "You must be terrified. I am sorry for that. Please excuse how rude we've been to you since you got here, but you must understand, we have been trapped inside here for a long, long time. Our entire race locked away for five hundred years, and you're the first person to arrive. We simply want to know how and figure it all out. You're hope to us, and new knowledge of the outside world we haven't seen in so long. You could get us out, back to the world your forefathers once lived in."

Whispers increase, spreading around the crowd like a breeze. I'm too speechless to say anything at all. I don't like where this is going. They want a saviour and I'm just not that. "Perhaps some rest and food would be best. You look exhausted. Then we can discuss more. There must be a clue." She looks back at Daegan.

He comes down the steps and offers me his arm. He smells like clean linen, the forest and cinnamon. "A beautiful lady should not walk alone. Please, let me escort you."

"I don't know you or trust you. Please, just let me go to see the door, and I can—"

"The door is gone. It was never there for anyone but you, and now that room is gone, too. The mansion wanted you here. The deities sent you to us, and I will make sure our gift is kept safe," he promises, still offering me his arm. I can't trust him. Trust is something I will never give easily ever again, but he might be my best shot at being protected here until I can escape.

I smile tensely at him and nod once. I don't have a choice and I want to get out of here, away from all the eyes watching me. I'm halfway across the room when I feel a heavy weight of someone's eyes on me that pulls my gaze over my shoulder, to the back of the room. A group of these people are sitting alone, and there's a male in the middle of them who draws all the attention. He's huge, taking up two of the seats easily, his thick arms stretched across the back. His messy black hair is cut short, shaved on each side, but wild on top. Moon-shaped earrings line his one ear, and they glitter in the moonlight that is shining on him. What looks like an actual black crescent moon marking lies on his right cheek.

He must be the most beguiling male I've ever seen. It's his eyes that near enough stop my legs from working. They're like molten silver fire, and they are focused on me with such intensity that his gaze sends shivers down my spine. Even at the back of the room, his stare is almost too much to hold, and his lips tilt up in a bit of a smirk, almost like he's sensing my reaction to him. His eyes might be beautiful, but they are cold, void of any warmth.

I can't help but notice how nobody sits next to his group. Their clothes are similar to the fae outside, black with silver-lined edges, but old-fashioned compared to the clothes worn in the cities. The rest of the groups here are in brighter, mostly yellow or orange colours. There's about twenty of them, sitting in a line up the steps, and not a single person goes anywhere near them. There are five or six empty seats separating the rest of the crowds from these people. It's on the tip of my tongue to ask Daegan who he is, but I don't, pulling my eyes away from the stranger, knowing I shouldn't stare long.

The second I look away, I sense something change in the room. It goes silent. Daegan pauses, and he turns back, anger written all over his face. When I follow his gaze, I find the man I saw a moment ago has stood. His arms are crossed, showing off dozens of dragon markings littered all over his hands and lower arms as his black shirt is rolled up. They are like Daegan's, but he has many more. The man looks at Daegan with clear disdain, and his voice is like honey gliding over my skin when he speaks. "The newcomer does not belong to you, Sun king. She is of age, and she will enter the Decidere."

Ripples of shocked gasps echo around the room.

"What's the Decidere?" I whisper to Daegan, but he hasn't taken his eyes off the man. I don't think I pronounced it right at all.

Daegan immediately defends me. "Ziven, she—"

"Enters the Decidere, or I will kill her myself. No fae belongs in our dynasties without earning their place." His tone is final. No one argues with him, and I don't blame them. He is terrifying and I'm a stranger. I don't know what the Decidere is, but I can tell it's not good. Ziven walks down the steps, purposely heading right towards me with his huge legs, and after the death threat, my own legs itch to run away. He's so tall, at least seven feet. Daegan isn't short by any means, but compared to Ziven, he seems it.

Ziven might kill me, and I haven't done anything with the life my best friend died to get me. I'm not brave like he said I was, and I don't even know how to be anything but a slave. Freedom, it is new and, so far, not all that amazing. I feel like a rat who escaped one trap only to run right into another, far worse one, and this time no one is going to protect me. My heart is in my throat as he walks right past me, followed by the twenty or so people he was with.

Only when they are gone does Daegan look down at me, and I feel like I can breathe. "I'm sorry. That was King Ziven Moonsilver of the Moon Dynasty, and he just demanded you enter a trial, one you arrived for right before it began. He never speaks in here, but he is another king, one of the few remaining, and I cannot refuse him without starting a war. He would like that."

"What is the Decidere?" I dare to ask. I don't care about their politics.

Daegan leads me to the door of the auditorium, and I'm glad for his arm as his words nearly destroy my ability to stand. "An ancient rite of passage for all fae over the age of twenty. Trials in the stones, which the dragons use to test your strength and choose if you will become a rider. Tomorrow, you will enter the trial with the others, and only the stone dragons below can help or shatter you."

KEEP READING WITH A VOW OF DRAGONS AND STORMS...

CHAPTER 18

Page Three.
We all have a calling, a longing
we are born to that makes our hearts
beat faster. If you're reading this,
you were called to a dragon, and it
is waiting for you. Make sure your
enemies don't kill you first.

We leave the auditorium before I can process anything he just said. Trials? Dragons? Stones? My head is swarming with questions and fears as we head into a deserted corridor, full of paintings of cities I've never seen and dragons that should be impossible. I want to stop in front of each one and ask about them, but Daegan doesn't slow down, and I get the feeling we shouldn't linger here. Daegan seems to follow my every look, reading my every expression and reaction to the paintings. There are windows every so often, and each one looks out into the forest, revealing nothing but rows of thick, tall trees. This place is hidden from the world, and I don't know how I found it. Why am I here?

We come to a stop before guarded doors with a huge sun symbol on the wood. The guards are wearing thick golden armour, and helmets completely cover their faces. They both bow to Daegan before opening the doors and letting us in.

Daegan's muscular shoulders drop a tad when the doors are shut behind us, and his pace does too. I end up just blurting out all of the questions swimming a storm up in my mind. "How do you even exist, Daegan? How is that possible to be trapped in here? Who trapped you? Where are your dragons? Are dragons even real? Will I be killed in the Decidere?"

Daegan waves ahead to a corridor that is also empty, but it's somehow warmer in here, not just the temperature but the yellow wallpaper, lush thick carpets, and soft furnishings that seem to invite you in. How big is this place? "I will answer every question you have, Story. Our dragons are real and alive. They are here, underground, below the mansion, and they cannot leave. Our dragons are just as trapped as we are. As for the Decidere, it is up to the deities and dragons if you die or not. Our people are proud to take the Decidere. It is an honour and there is a chance you will bond with a dragon. Even if you aren't seen as worthy of a dragon, the Decidere will help you grow as a person and find who you are. Who your soul is when it's pushed to the extreme. When you let us out into the world, we'll be going to war, with our dragons leading the way, burning the skies and vampyres to dust."

That thought is horrifying. "If your people have not left in five hundred years, how old are you, exactly? How many generations have lived in here? Do you even know what it's like outside?"

He laughs softly. "Story, I imagine we will have many talks over our meals in the months to come. All these questions…which do you want answered first, as each question holds a long answer."

My cheeks brighten under his stare. He is… nice. That's my first impression of the Sun Dynasty king, but I know not to trust the nice people. Usually, they are far worse than the ones who show you they are assholes to begin with. When I don't answer him, he links his hands together behind his back. "The vampyres, have they taken our cities?"

I frown. "I think they warped history, as I don't know any cities that were not built by the vampyres. They like to have us believe that we fae were wild and untamed before they stepped in, that they helped us and we owe them for that. The vampyres rule with an iron fist, and no one escapes their laws if they are born fae." He waits for my every word, and I don't know what to make of it. "The vampyres have five grand cities. They're basically run by the fae to benefit the vampyres. I was born in the breeding district, within the Nightwell city, which is the capital and the largest. It is south of here, actually. Just outside the forest by a few hundred miles."

His voice is thick. "Please, carry on."

"Well, when fae are born, they are usually born into the breeder communities, but there are exceptions born into the others—the blood slaves and the workers. Every fae baby is sent to the breeders' nursery to be fed, brought up and adopted by other families if they don't have parents or family in the breeders. 'The lessborn fae' are what they call us. Every lessborn fae is tested for powers when they are born, just to make sure they don't belong with the powerborn fae. If you are powerborn, you'd be taken to the powerborn district nursery. For powerborn fae, they basically train to be what their family needs or what their power develops as. Healers, those who give warrior vampyres their powers, those who control the elements to help grow crops and those who can control the mind are used by the royals to find spies and more. I don't know much more. I was never in that part very much."

"I dislike that name 'lessborn,'" he all but snarls at me, and he blinks, softening his voice. "No fae is less than incredible, including you." No one has called me incredible before. I guess he really doesn't know me. "You told me you were a blood slave. What does that mean?"

"Vampyres have their own system. The

nobility—vampyres of exceptional skill, genius or battle skills—are given a fae to feed on as they see fit. The others go to places where the workers and breeders mass donate blood for them to drink. Vampyres only need a glassful a day to survive. I had two owners. One was kind and one was—" I nearly choke on the memories of him. "Not."

Daegan watches me closely, a frown promptly pulling his lips down. Somehow, he doesn't look less handsome frowning. He opens a wooden door, leading me into a well lit room. Four large lanterns hang from the corners of the room, and it's pretty in here. A lot of things are gold, shaped like suns, and I'm getting the general vibe of this place. A massive, plush sun-shaped mat lies in the middle of the room, with a dark wooden desk on it. There's an oil lamp on the desk, plush yellow chairs, and couches around the edges of the room with small tables at their sides. There are several books piled up on the desk, and my fingers itch to rush over, to open them, and to know their secrets. My mother always said I was as nosy as the diamond cat-like creature that stalked the mice in our garden. I guess she was right.

Daegan closes the door behind me, and I hold in my flinch as it shuts. He waits until I take a seat on one of the chairs before he sits in the one opposite, crossing one leg over the other. "I'm sure you're curious about what is going to happen next. I have asked my second-in-command to call a meeting between our dynasties to speak about you. I will be on your side, and I plan to make sure you will be kept in my dynasty, safe for the remainder of the Decidere. But I need to know everything that led you to here so I can convince them I am asking you the right questions."

Rubbing my hands together, I tell him everything as I stare at my mud-soaked leggings. The mud is everywhere, all the way up to my waist, and it's now gone dry, cracking as I move. There's mud on my hands, my bare feet and there's even some splattered on my face and hair as I sit in front of a king who apparently rides a dragon. My mother would be horrified, but I can barely even remember what her voice sounds like now.

While I talk about running through the forest that I researched ahead of time, Daegan pours water into a teapot. He covers the pot with his hands, and I swear they glow for a second before he takes his hands away. He pours two cups from the pot and brings the steaming drinks over, handing me one. "It's camomile and lemon balm, it helps—"

"I know." It's hard to hold back my tears as I look at the drink. He was trying to be kind, not make me cry. "My best friend was the son of a healer, and his mother used to make me the same tea from her gardens on my bad days. It helped calm me."

Daegan sips on his tea as he leans on the desk. He doesn't ask about the bad days, and he likely thinks I mean from the vampyre who owned me. No, bad days are where my body feels like it's being ripped apart once every six months due to my monthlies, whereas the days made bad by my owner were just another day. "And where is he? This friend of yours? Will he come after you? Will any family?"

"He's dead and no," I barely whisper. "I don't want to talk about him anymore." I can't. I won't tell this stranger about my mother either.

"I understand. My brother died not ten years ago, and I thought there would never be a day my voice wouldn't break when I spoke about him, but here we are," he confidently tells me, and I meet his gold eyes. "Understand, Story, it's not safe in here for you. You came here at an interesting time, right before the Decidere, which hasn't been done in years because of the wars between our dynasties. We are at peace now, have been for nine years, but it's in our nature to become explosive and violent creatures when caged."

Never cage a wolf, my mother once said, because once their mind has rotted, there are only teeth which promise death. "Explain it to me. Some of the way that you live. You're the Sun Dynasty king, and you said that Ziven was the Moon Dynasty king. Are there others?"

"There were five dynasties once, before the doom. The doom is the day our ancestors got trapped in here, and the dragons too," he explains as I drink the tea. I know I'm going to need more than tea to calm my beating heart and soothe the thunder in my veins. "Three kings ruled our many cities. Sun, Moon, and Dawn Dynasties. The Twilight Dynasty and Dusk Dynasty were killed off years ago in wars, years before the doom, and their people scattered between our own. In here, I rule. The Sun

Dynasty is in charge and has been for years since Ziven left us alone after the last war. My older brother was happy to rule and taught me everything I needed to know before he died. We needed a ruler."

"And Dawn?" I ask, thoroughly interested in their politics now. If I'm stuck in here, which I'm getting the feeling I am as I haven't seen a door to leave yet, I need to learn as much as I can to keep myself safe.

"The Dawn Dynasty is here in small numbers, like the Moon Dynasty, but their ruler is not interested in ruling. He wants peace and, most importantly, a way out of here. I'm sure he might finally lift his head out of his books to come and meet you when he hears."

I might join him with the books. "So, the dynasties are based on the day and night? Dawn, Sun, and Moon? Do you all share this mansion and live together?"

"Correct, but we live apart in some sense. Our power comes from our dynasty. Sunlight is my power," he answers, rising to his feet and coming to me. He takes my empty cup, putting them both back on the tray by the pot. "This mansion is far bigger than it looks, with over three thousand rooms. I rule everywhere except for the Moon Dynasty floor, the bottom floor of the mansion before the caves. I will ask that you don't go down there, but other than that rule, you're free to walk around. I will insist someone is with you for the beginning if I'm not around myself. You're new to us, and we were never good at trusting strangers."

"Then why are you helping me?"

He looks at the desk, at the book lying open. "I was reading a story when you arrived about a saviour of our people, and I felt the mansion shake right under my feet. I felt compelled to find you, and I'm trusting that feeling. I was meant to help you."

"Can I read it?" I question. He smiles, picking the book up and handing it to me. I run my finger across the leather binding before tightening my grip around my new book. It's been so long since I read a new book, not just re-read the same books on vampyres. "Are you sure you don't mind me borrowing it?"

"Don't tell me the ending, Story."

I smile back at him. He is charming, and he has given me a book. In any other circumstances, this would make us great friends. "You never answered my question about how old you are. I know some powerborn fae can live a lot longer than others. Hundreds of years, apparently."

"Yes, we can," he answers me, but still not at the same time. He barely looks like he's more than thirty years old, but appearances can be deceiving. "To grow old in here is a lucky circumstance. Unfortunately, there is something in here that attacks us, kills us. A sickness that spreads from touch. Once you have it, it's impossible to survive. It took both my father and my mother. We haven't seen the sickness in eight years, so you're fine right now."

Another thing to worry about. Great. "I'm sorry for your loss."

"But you're here. It has to mean something," he repeats with hope burning in his voice like the sun, and I already don't like the pressure I feel from him. He thinks I'm a magic ticket out of here. He is going to lose it when he realises I'm a worthless blood slave fae who isn't fantastic at anything. The door's knocked twice and Daegan pulls his eyes from me to the door. "Come in, Etena."

She walks in, holding the door slightly ajar. "Her room is ready."

Daegan nods and offers me his hand to help me up. I take it and notice how warm he is to touch. "I think perhaps it's best if you rest and have a bath. Etena is my cousin, and she will show you the way. I am in the room opposite you. If you need anything, just knock."

I let go of his hand, noticing I've been clasping onto it for far too long. "Thank you for offering to protect me. You don't even know me. Where I come from, people don't help strangers."

Daegan inclines his head. "Rest well, Story."

Etena opens the door for me, and I walk out, waiting for her as she quietly speaks to Daegan out of earshot before she comes back, shutting the door behind her. The very tall woman places her hands on her hips, looking me over. "Did you run through a mud lake on your way here?"

"Just the forest, no lake," I answer, but she is already moving, walking down a pathway that arches into a circular room. There are three enormous fireplaces made of brick, in square-shaped blocks in the centre, with many, many benches, couches and lush rugs that have people sitting on them—fae-tipped ears and all—and they are laughing. The laughter slowly stops the further I follow Etena into the room, noticing the many, many heads turning to stare. Etena moves faster across the room until we are in another corridor, and the sound of chatter still follows us.

"Did Daegan explain you're safe here?" she questions. "In this part of the mansion."

"He told me," I simply answer. I'm exhausted and done with conversation tonight. I need to process everything that just happened and figure out exactly how I'm going to get out of here before they throw me into the Decidere. I'm not built for trials or dragons or any kind of combat. I've never been trained to fight and, knowing me, I'd stab myself with a sword before learning how to swing it at an enemy. We head down the corridors, which are not so empty now, but anyone here steps aside, all giving me strange looks. I can't imagine what it must be like to them—to never see someone new except a baby. Actually... "Where are the children? I haven't seen any."

She answers quickly. "Kept safely away

318

during the Decidere. It isn't for children to see."
Etena opens a door. This one is guarded like
Daegan's study, and the guards step aside for us
to go through. "These are the royal bedrooms.
Only you, Daegan, and I sleep here. If you see
anyone else in here, run. Kill them if you have
to. Daegan would kill them either way for
entering his private rooms."

I gulp. "Kill them?"

She turns to face me, crossing her slender
arms. "Yes, kill them? Why do you look so pale
at the idea?" I don't answer her with the truth.
I've never killed anyone, I don't like blood, and
I'm not brave. I'm not a fucking warrior. "You
don't have to talk to me if you don't want to,
Story. I understand trauma very well, and
looking in your eyes, I know you've been
through a lot already. I have a soft spot for
people like us."

"Like us?" I frown.

"Survivors. One day, we will exchange our
battle stories, cry over them, and bond like
friends. Tonight is not the time while you're
tired and injured," she answers, and bonding
with anyone seems really unlikely for me when
I want to get out of here, run away and pretend

none of this happened. How does she know I'm injured? I've been hiding my pain since I got here, something I know I'm good at. "Telling you to trust me is pointless, isn't it?"

I raise an eyebrow. "I don't trust people. I don't trust anyone." Except one person and he is dead. He died to set me free. He died for nothing. My fingers tighten on the book to the point it creaks. I don't mean to be hostile towards her, but today has pushed every inch of my soul to the breaking point. I've not even had a moment to grieve my best friend, my only friend in the world, and how he's just gone. He's gone and he won't be coming back. I'm not sure how I'll ever be able to process that. I only need to try to protect myself and not give up. I can't go back to that dark place I was before my best friend promised to get me out. I gave up on life, I gave up on wanting to fight or live or breathe, and right now that feeling is crawling up my spine, readying to flood my mind with the darkness again. Without him, I know I won't be able to climb out of that place.

Giving up isn't an option. Not anymore, not since he died. Etena touches my shoulder, and I focus on the present, on her. "I left some clothes on your bed for you, and I ran a healing bath. We don't get hot water in here, it's lukewarm, but…it's better than nothing. The water has tonics in it made by the Sun healers with dragon tears, and it heals everything."

Dragon tears?

"Welcome to the Sun Dynasty, Story," Etena says, bowing her head. "I believe you're going to surprise us all, more than you already have." Etena walks away, leaving through the doors we came in. This pathway has four doors, one I'm in front of, and the one opposite must be Daegan's. The carpet is worn, like it's been walked on dozens of times, and so is the carpet near the door next to mine, but the areas around the fourth door and mine look almost new.

I walk into the room and shut the door behind me, noticing a flimsy lock, and I click it shut. If these fae are as strong as the powerborn fae, that lock will do nothing to stop them getting in, but I feel better either way. The room is simple, yellow wallpaper like the hallways and wooden cladding panels, which line half the walls. An oil lantern burns on the bedside counter, and I see the bed has soft white sheets as I place the book on the counter. There's a window, and I go straight over, looking for a handle, but there's nothing. Just a dark-rimmed window with lines down it in a cross pattern, revealing nothing but dark trees as far as I can see. I touch the glass. "Why did you trap me in here? What do you want?"

I'm talking to a mansion wall. I've gone mad. Muttering to myself, I strip my mud-soaked clothes off before climbing into the simmering clear bath, soaking down into the warmth. The pain melts away almost instantly from my ribs, from every small nick and bruise I have on me. I sink fully into the water before rising back out, my swollen cut lip back to normal. My heart is beating fast as I look down at my stomach, my wrists, and legs…hoping the vampyre bite scars will be gone—they aren't. The silver scars look as horrible as usual, and not an inch of my skin on my stomach, lower arms or legs doesn't have a mark on them. He may have scarred me, but I'm free of him.

The bath doesn't last long before it's freezing cold, and I wash my hair with the lavender-scented soap that smells incredible. After climbing out, I glance at the clothes on the bed as I dry myself off. The gold silky top pulls across my chest, and strips of satin fall down my upper arms. Skin-tight black trousers and clean leather boots, along with new underwear that is all lace—I slide them on, admiring the delicate material and the fact it all perfectly fits. This is much better than a red dress. I haven't had a choice in what I wear in so long, and if I'm being honest with myself, I've only ever known how to dress for my station. Red, for a blood slave. It has made me really hate wearing red.

I find a brush on the side and brush my long hair until it's smooth and all the knots from the forest are gone. I braid the front part of my hair around my face until it falls to one side.

Once I have nothing left to do, I climb into the bed with the book, opening the first page. It's an odd book, no title page to be seen in the first few blank pages. The first page is noted and one sentence: "To my reader—I was a dragon rider, and if you're reading this, I must be dead." How strange. There is a name scribbled in the corner, but I can only make out the letter *B*, the rest is scrubbed away. The next pages are the same, one or two sentences about someone who was a dragon rider and something about stones. I like mysteries, and this book is that.

I close my eyes for just a second, my head dropping. I see his face, pure terror and horror written in his eyes. I see his blood pouring onto the stone. A sob echoes out of my throat first, right before I'm weeping and sliding down into the bedsheets. I don't know how long I cry, at least until it feels like I can breathe again. Wiping my tears away with my hand, I pause as a floorboard creaks. I barely get to look up from under my blanket before I see a shadow standing over my bed, massive male arms reaching for me. On instinct, I kick the man straight in the balls, and his deep, shocked voice echoes. "FUCK!"

He steps back with a groan, and I rush off the bed, running for the door. A hand wraps around my ankle, and I fall face-first on the floorboards, slamming my nose into the ground. I cry out in pain only for a foul-smelling rag to be shoved over my mouth. I barely breathe in the air for a second before everything spins and the darkness becomes a very welcome old friend.

CHAPTER 19

Page Four.

I was born to the Lightsun city, and I grew up in piles of gold, silver, and jewels sent by the Sun Dynasty for all royal fae children no matter which dynasty they were born, but my heart...it called to the dark. To the moon, and he was my ruin.

I stand before a row of vampyres. Each of them looks nearly the same to me. Same grey or very pale skin, white cloaks, white hats, fangs flashing every time *they talk—scientists. Vampyres, not very high up ones, but people trained for district selection day. Blaire told me they would only double-check what she had found out, make a detailed file on my health, age, and anything my new owner would want to know before I would be taken to the preference housing. Two dark-haired girls next to me are crying hysterically, and the other two boys are completely silent. I wonder what is wrong with their health, why they are here with me. They are all a similar age to me, but not from the breeders' camp I grew up in. I don't know how many camps there are, but my mother once mentioned there were many.*

I can't help the tears from rolling down my face when I think of my mother, of how she held me and said goodbye. How she looked broken and sad—and there wasn't anything either of us could do to fix it. My body is shaking from head to toe, but it's not cold in here, it's actually warmer than expected in winter. I keep my head up, my shoulders straight, just like my mother told me to do before she left me with Blaire. They both promised me that everything would be okay. That was three days ago, and now I'm going to be taken to a hellhole to be picked like a fruit hanging from a tree. For nothing more than a snack whenever he wants one. Or she. I am hoping for a woman. She might be kinder.

The door opens and all the scientists turn and look as a man walks in. He has curly locks of hair, very pale skin, and he is older. Vampyres age slowly and this man has grey-tinted red hair and a wrinkle on his forehead like he has been frowning too often. His skin is completely drained of any colour, a grey so light it could be white. His eyes are brown, unusual for a vampyre from what I've seen in the breeder communities, the few I've seen when they come round to do their checks. All of the guards never take off their helmets, but there are vampyres who come to visit fae women who are paid to see them without armour. I didn't need my mother to tell me why they visit. The horror in her voice was a story enough, and she always hid me when they came.

There's a pin clipped to this vampyre's cloak, and I don't recognise the symbol. It's a broken hammer, gold on red. The vampyre speaks to one scientist, nodding his head towards me. The scientist turns once and raises his hand to me, indicating for me to walk over. Sickness rises in my throat as I force my legs to move, and I stop next to them both. "You are coming with me, Story Dehana. Don't fight or I will have them inject you to sleep, and you will still come with me."

His voice is sharp, clipped, and every time he speaks, I see a hint of ruby red fangs. Why are his fangs red like that? I don't know how my legs manage to work as I follow him out of the room, down old stone corridors and out into the busy streets. There's a brown, highly decorated carriage waiting, two white horses tied to the front, and a fae driver sitting on the seat. I only see his fae ears tipping out of his brown hat and his brown clothes. He is a worker.

The vampyre opens the door for me, and I step in before plastering myself to the back of the carriage seat. He steps in after me, and the carriage takes off the second the door is shut. He looks down at his hand before reaching forward and touching the sides of the carriage. I smell magic as it whips through the air, washing over the carriage until there's almost a shimmery shine on the windows. Magic smells like ash, like something has burnt to a crisp and blown through the air. "We can speak freely now and no one will hear us, courtesy of my driver, a very talented fae who is not meant to have any powers. That will be kept between us, alright?"

Why is he telling me a secret? He doesn't know me. "O-okay?"

He picks up a pocket watch from his suit pocket, looking at the time before sliding it back. "Story, I don't expect you to trust me, but Blaire asked for a favour. Blaire, I owe her a great deal. She keeps a lot of secrets for me, which you will have to do as well, living in my house. I was told you can be trusted, just like your mother."

My voice is too high pitched as I manage to speak. "Did you know my father?"

His eyes flash with something, but he looks away from me. "No. My name is Professor Aleksander Wollke, and you are a blood slave to me now. I have no others. I have never needed to take one, and frankly, I find the whole idea cruel and unneeded. When I want to feed, I usually just get blood from the docks, but I won't be able to do that now. I will not feed from you directly, but it has to come across that I do. I have no intention of hurting you."

"Why?" *I whisper. A vampyre that doesn't*

want to hurt a fae? My mother told me they didn't exist.

"Because it's cruel and you are a person. I have tools in my home ready, and they will make it easy for you to pierce your arm and drain blood into a glass for me. I will drink that, but if anyone asks, you are bitten when I want to feed, do you understand?"

I nod. "Yes."

"In my house, you'll be safe, and blood slaves are relatively safe around the city when you go out. You'll need to wear these and the colour red at all times." He hands me two silver bracelets. They have his name written on them, and also a symbol.

The hammer symbol again. "What does this mean?"

He looks away from me. "I work in the palace." My blood goes ice cold. "I make metal work for the royal soldiers, with the powerborn fae under my command. My estate is just outside the castle. It's tiny, but it's nothing for you to be concerned about living in. You'll be able to enter the city with the carriage whenever you wish. I will not bring you into the castle, so you have nothing to fear from the royals."

"Why should I trust you?" I ask after a long pause.

"Because your mother trusted Blaire, and Blaire loved your father," he bluntly informs me. She loved him. *"I will keep you safe."*

Little does the professor know, or I know at this time, that by picking me, he would never, ever be able to keep me safe.

I wake up to the sound of light tapping, like rain pinging off a glass window. Lifting my head, I first see a massive black boot in front of me as I breathe in the smell of whatever is still on my skin. There is a foul taste in my mouth that reminds me of the man who kidnapped me from my room and shoved a cloth into my face. It's an herbal scent, and my eyes are burning from it. I draw my eyes up his immense body to come face to face with King Ziven as he towers over me, his thick arms crossed, tight black shirt and heavy dark trousers. He was the man in my room. His black hair is just as messy as when we met, locks of it falling down his forehead as his silver eyes watch me. No mercy, no empathy. There is nothing but bitter hostility lingering in his weighted gaze. He leans down and before I can blink, there's a silver dagger pressed directly to my throat, the tip cutting the skin just underneath my chin. "Give me a reason not to kill you."

That should be an easy answer for most people. Most people would say their loved ones' names, speak of the future they planned out or the dream they want to live. The problem is, I don't exactly have a reason, other than the very basic, the obvious answer. "I want to live, but I won't beg. I promised myself that I'd never beg a king again."

His eyes darken, the silver going impossibly grey. "What king could you know before me and Daegan? Has he had you begging already?"

I won't tell him anything, but that slip of the tongue was a mistake. He can kill me if he wants, I can't tell him more. "Killing me is not going to get you anything that you want." He pushes the dagger into my neck, nipping my skin. I gasp. "Killing me will just leave you trapped in here."

He smiles at my bluff, like he got exactly what he wanted. I don't know why I just said that. "You do know exactly how you got in here, little liar?" He grabs the back of my neck and lifts me up to him. Somehow, he doesn't hurt me more with the dagger as he leans down over me until our faces are inches apart. There's nothing but fury written in his eyes. "You come in here on the night of the greatest storm I've ever seen and cause trouble, unrest through our people. I was going to let you live until you tried to blackmail me with your knowledge."

"I-I wasn't—"

"Don't lie to me, Storm," he sneers. "Knowledge like that is going to get you killed."

His breath mixes with mine with how close he is holding me to his body, only an inch apart. He smells like stormy nights full of rain, a deep masculine oakmoss and lime scent and everything forbidden. He makes it hard to focus. "I told you all the truth. Etena would have known if I lied."

"Etena can see when someone lies, but it does not mean she can't lie to protect Daegan's interests." Ziven runs the dagger up my chin, up my cheek and back down. "It would be so easy to plunge this dagger into your heart and stop it all before it goes too far."

"Stop what?" I breathe out. He lets me go. I finally feel like I can move as he takes a step back, blinking more than once, his long dark eyelashes fluttering. Now the dagger's not on my throat, and his hand's not burning into the back of my neck, everything feels a little less intense. He walks away from me and sits down on a chair, a single chair in the dark room we are in. Oil lanterns burn on the walls, but they burn silver, casting a strange light upon both of us. He leans elbow on his knee and watches me like he is bored. We say nothing for a long time, and I wonder how long I've been in here. Will anyone come for me, or will he let me go? "Tell me a secret, Storm."

"My name is Story Dehana, and I am proud of my name. It is not *Storm*," I answer, lifting my head high even when all I want to do is bang the walls, beg for someone to save me from him. I'm shaking again and I hate how much he can see it. He must think I'm weak. "And I have no secrets that would interest you."

"We both know you're lying. I don't need the precious Etena to tell me that," he smirks. I glance at the moon mark on his cheek. How it moves slightly, like it's alive. The dragons on his hands and arms move too, flying slowly around. He follows my gaze, and I snap my eyes up. "Ask."

"What are those marks? What is your power?" I blurt out.

His eyes are nothing but amused. "You wouldn't want to know what my power is, and I said ask. I didn't say I wished to be your tutor, Storm."

That nickname again. "Can't be that great if you're trapped in here with the rest of them," I snap and instantly regret the words when his eyes bleed of all amusement, leaving pure anger. *Shut up, Story. For the love of the deities, don't wind this king up.* I lift my hands in the air. "Look, I'm sorry about hitting you in the balls, but you were kidnapping me, so I feel like that was your fault, too. I'm going to go, because apparently you demanded I go do some kind of crazy ass trial thing, and I don't want to do that, but I doubt I'm getting a choice."

"You're going to walk straight out the door, Storm?" He sits straighter. "Tell me how you did that. Did the king you knew tell you we were here and sent you to be a spy to kill us all?"

My mouth parts. "No! Deities above, no!" I shake my head. "And it's *Story*. I don't appreciate nicknames, and I'm not a spy."

"While you continue to lie to me, you will be called whatever I wish, Storm."

I snap my teeth together. "Fine, call me whatever you want. I'm no liar."

He laughs, a cruel, taunting laugh. "Everyone is a liar. You're going to tell me your secrets and exactly how you got in here, why you're here, and if you take one step against us, I'll make sure your death is painful. Your king will only get your ashes back."

He's insane. Completely insane.

"King Ziven, we don't know each other, but I don't want an enemy. I'm not here to—"

"More lies." He waves a hand, cutting me off. "I was told about how you believe you have no powers. Lessborn? What a bullshit name."

That might be the only thing we agree on. "I'm not powerborn—"

Suddenly light shines in from behind me, and I turn just in time to see a wall literally collapsing on itself, bright burning golden light shining in through it. Daegan steps in and the light is coming from his hands, pure sunlight. He looks me over, clearly checking for injuries, and walks straight to my side. His hand rests on my back, and it's a possessive move that I see

Ziven smirk at. I'm not sure I like it, because we barely know each other, but he might get me away from Ziven, so I don't move. "Do you want to start a war, Ziven?"

"Are you suggesting we have a war? The last was fun," Ziven answers, casually leaning back.

Daegan clenches his jaw. "*Fun* is not a word I would use for the deaths. Our peace treaty is simply paper, easily burnt in the light, and you know what that would mean."

They both look at each other. Ziven yawns. "You're not the only one that gets to keep her like a pretty doll you've picked up from a shop. I don't see any sun marks on her hands, on her cheeks or neck. Therefore, she's not yours. I did not break any part of our treaty. Have you even dared to ask her to be in your dynasty yet?"

"The treaty has no part about fae outside the dynasties," Daegan responds. "She is coming with me, if she wants to."

"I do," I answer quickly.

Ziven only winks at me. "Go then. She's not going to talk yet, but I'm sure the Decidere will loosen her tongue. If she survives the first day, then she spends half her week here, in my dynasty, so she can make a choice of her own. That's my offer."

It sounds like there is an "or else" missing at the end of his words. "I didn't know I was up for discussion about where I lived here."

Daegan glances at me, his voice softer. "There are old laws from the fae. Back before the doom, when a fae turned eighteen, they would spend six months in each dynasty so they might choose where they wanted to pledge to. Once pledged in blood to a dynasty, you cannot change."

"And what if I don't want to do that and just be me?" I question. "No dynasty."

Ziven laughs at me, and my cheeks brighten. "We can go back to the previous topic of war. You'd be the first one I'd kill."

Deities above, he is a lunatic. Daegan gives in pretty quickly to Ziven, most likely to protect me. "Fine, we'll be leaving, and I agree to your terms. Her trial's only an hour away now, as you've had her all night."

"All night?" I gasp. "But—"

"Leave my dynasty," Ziven interrupts me, and I bite down on my tongue before I snap at him, at this powerful king. Daegan leads me out, but before I get to the broken wall, Ziven's voice echoes to me. "Your secrets will come out one way or the other, Storm. I look forward to breaking you."

I look over my shoulder, watching him as I walk away, deciding right here and now that I hate him. Ziven is an asshole. We walk out over the broken pieces of brick and down a corridor, past several archways. I can't help but look in through the open doors, spotting that everything here isn't exactly golden like I've seen. There are dark wood floors, silver wallpaper, the silver couches lining the walls, and matching plush armchairs that face the enormous fireplaces.

We come to a guarded door that must be the way out of the Moon Dynasty, and instead of the gold-plated armoured guards Daegan has by his doors, the two female fae standing there are both dressed casually. I would guess they're twins, with their matching black hair and beautiful features. I couldn't tell them apart if I tried. They hold the door open, both impassive as we step through, and they shut it behind us. The corridor is all golden out here, from the carpets to the walls, and Daegan doesn't say anything until we've walked quite far. Only when we come out to a balcony on the second floor does he take his hand away from my back.

I can't hear him as I look at the massive statue in the middle of the mansion. It's huge, with wings spread out to make pathways on the top floor, and the fae walk across them. There are ten floors by my count, all with balconies and pathways around the dragon leaping for the ceiling, its nose touching the top of the ceiling where a crack is spread across it. Almost like this dragon was trying to escape and it got frozen in time. "I'm extremely sorry. I didn't think he'd have the balls to come in and take you."

He makes me laugh for only a second as I think about the fact I hit Ziven in the balls. I'm not sure if Daegan would find that funny. "It's not your fault. I'm not in your dynasty, and we've only known each other a day or so. You don't owe me anything."

"I promised you protection, Story," he bites out. His anger is directed at the Moon king, not me, but he frightens me for a second. "It's not as easy as you think to find you in that place, but I want you to know I was looking for you all night."

"Thank you for coming for me," I answer with a tense smile. I really hope he doesn't think I owe him anything. "You didn't have to do that."

He stands, looking at the dragon with me. "I did."

People walk past us as I touch the banister, the metal cold and soothing. "What would happen if there was a war between you two? I don't want to cause that."

"We don't get along. There's history— family history—between us," he hedges. "It means that we'll never be friends. Ziven took you to piss me off, to show that he can if he wants to. He knows I am interested in how you got in here, and want to find a way out. Whereas Ziven? I'm not sure he ever wants to leave."

"Why wouldn't he want to leave?"

He looks at me like he wants to tell me more, but a bell rings softly. "I want to show you somewhere before I take you to the beginning of the Decidere. We've only got three quarters of an hour, I'm afraid."

I look down at my clothes. "Is what I'm wearing appropriate for this?"

"It's fine," Daegan answers as we walk

away from the balcony and to a massive staircase that wraps tightly around the body of the
dragon, all the way up to its wings. He takes me
back to his apartments, to my room on the top
floor, where I use the bathroom and quickly
freshen up before he walks me down to what I
think is the eighth floor. There are three
massive archway doors, almost like small
tunnels with lines drawn into the stone, and we
head through one into one of the biggest rooms
I've ever seen. Each tall wall is lined with
books on shelves, and they are a rainbow of
colours. My mouth pops open. There must be
hundreds of thousands, if not more, books on at
least twenty levels of this gigantic room. There
are many tables around the floor with oil
lanterns burning, but this entire library is
empty.

Daegan clears his throat. "I got the feeling
you like books. I'm not a huge reader, but my
mother was, and she loved this place. You're
free to come here whenever you want and read
whatever you wish, but we insist on the books
being put back once they've been taken out of
here. We try to preserve this library; it is all the
books we have left from our cities. The ten

grand libraries of the dynasties…and these are all that is left of the stories of the world."

A single tear falls down my cheek, and I don't notice it until Daegan wipes it away, resting his hand on my cheek for a few moments. He shakes his head, stepping back. "Do you like it?"

"Like? I *love* it," I whisper in awe. "It's like a dream."

He smiles so brightly, and I realise that he is handsome. So, so handsome. "I thought it would give you a reason to survive for me. All the books that you can read if you survive today." He searches my eyes. "I know that you feel probably like you're trapped in here with us, but there's something good about being trapped here. We can find the light for you." I wrap my arms around his neck, hugging him tightly and even surprising myself. He seems surprised too for a second, before he hugs me back just as tightly.

I'm blushing as I pull back. "Thank you."

He tucks a strand of my loose hair behind my ear, so casually, like he has done it a million times. "Give them a reason to write a story about you and survive the Decidere."

CHAPTER 20

Page Five.
The stones are the traps.
Run to the unknown; it is your
only hope.

rums echo from below, and the lower we climb down the staircase, the more they seem to vibrate the ground under my feet. I'm terrified. I thought the bravest thing I ever did was trying to escape with my best friend, but he got killed and I wasn't brave enough when it counted. My owner told me I was a coward, and he was right. I'm surprised my legs haven't stopped working yet.

Somehow, I keep descending the stairs with hundreds of other people. Many of them step aside once they see Daegan, while others don't seem to notice him, but their heads swing to look at me. They're so different from the fae that I've seen, but being stared at isn't something massively new to me. This time, they are curious, and there is a mixture of pity and desire on their faces that I am getting used to. There's something different about these fae, but I can't put my finger on what it is.

When we get down to the bottom level, which has no flooring, just stone, there's a drawn-out pathway right to the middle where there are at least a hundred people waiting in lines. Daegan leads me to the front, stopping me in the space that's been left open between others waiting. Daegan rests his hands on my shoulders. "Good luck," he tells me, leaning in. "You can do this."

No, I really can't. I do not know who he thinks I am, but I am not the right person to do any of this. I'm not sure exactly what *this* even is. My heart's racing as I look at what is clearly a cavern entrance in front of me. There's a single door, with a massive stone dragon on the smooth front, two more stone dragon statues on either side. Everything is quiet as Daegan walks towards a small platform in front of the doors. Etena meets him and they talk quietly between each other. As more people gather, I glance to my left to see a long, dark-haired, very curvy woman staring at me with her bright blue eyes sparkling like she is going to burst if she doesn't say something. She's about the same age as me, and her cheeks go bright red when I smile at her. "Hi, Story."

"Hello," I whisper back.

She looks around before grinning at me, and her smile is contagious. "Everyone's talking about you. I didn't, I wasn't there because I work in the libraries and my ladder fell down. I was stuck five floors up until they came back, but my sister came rushing back to tell me all about you. I can't believe you're standing next to me!"

I like her. "Nice to meet you. I've just seen the library. It's amazing. What's your name?"

"Oh, I can't believe I didn't introduce myself. I'm Catherine." She bows her head, and I see a sun marking on her neck. I bow my head back, wondering if that's how people greet each other in here. Fae aren't allowed to greet or speak to each other in the vampyre cities, but in the breeding sections, we always clasp our arms. "It's really nice to meet you."

"Same," I tell her back.

Her voice dips so quiet that I can barely hear her. "Is it true that you're going to find a way to get us out of here?" It's on the tip of my tongue to say no, that I'm a random fool who ran into a creepy abandoned mansion to escape the vampyres hunting me and it was an accident. She likely knows that part of the story if her sister was in the auditorium. I open my lips to say something and then close them again. "It's okay, you probably shouldn't tell me anyway. I'm a nobody librarian assistant, and you're... well, the hope of our people."

Hope of our people? Fuck, that sounds like a pressure-filled title I never asked for. What happens to me when they realise that I'm clueless and can't even get myself out? "I think being an assistant librarian is a brilliant job. I'd love to do that."

"Really?" she whispers, her eyes wide. "It's not paid, but I love it too. They are always looking for new assistants. Maybe if we both survive this, I could ask for you?"

I nod, my heart leaping. Another reason to try to survive today—other than the fact I don't want to die. Not yet. "Isn't it amazing the Decidere is finally open? It's been so many years. I've been hearing the call for ten years, like so many of us that signed up. Many are still waiting, of course, because not everyone's allowed to enter."

"Not everyone has to do this?" I sharply ask, not bothering to whisper this time. A rite of passage for fae, my ass.

She looks down at the ground. "No. It's only us that want to, who feel a calling. I think they assumed you felt the calling too, turning up on the day you did. The auditorium was full of us, the fae who applied and were waiting, when King Daegan carried you in."

Daegan carried me in. He also lied to me about this being a rite of passage and gave into what Ziven demanded. Catherine looks up and over my shoulder, quickly diverting her gaze at whatever she sees. I turn to see people parting, like a skipping stone being thrown across the water. Ziven walks in, as casual as always, when his eyes promise death to anyone that stands in his way. I don't get why they are so clearly frightened of him, other than his obvious fuck-off demeanour. The Sun Dynasty clearly has more people than the Moon, so why are they feared?

He is followed by the rest of his people, all twenty of them. They gather behind him, and Ziven looks over his shoulder, and a man steps to his side. The man is immense like Ziven, but his arms are bigger, his head is completely shaved, and instead of hair, there is a moon marking on his head. Ziven nods at him once, patting his shoulder, and then he purposely looks at me. They both do. The man leaves Ziven, and it looks like he's walking straight towards me as my heart races. Did Ziven tell this man to kill me before I enter the Decidere? I wouldn't put it past him. The man walks up right behind me, shoving the poor man who was there before out of the way with a grunt before taking his place in the line so he can loom over me like a shadow.

I quickly shoot my head forward, feeling eyes burning into the back of my head, and sweat trickles down my spine. Why do I feel like I'm being set up here? Daegan lets out a beam of light from his hand, and thousands of sparks fly around the room before shooting straight back into his hands. Pretty trick. The crowd goes silent.

"Welcome. It's been too long since we've allowed newcomers into the stone caves and opened the Decidere. Each one of you has been called to this, heard the dragons below, and proved your soul as strong." I did none of that. "This is a special year for all of us." His eyes rest on me for a second before looking around the crowd. "And I'm sure the deities are watching down on us, blessing our flights and battles. The dragons live below, and they are wild creatures. Never forget this. This is their home, their personal hunting grounds. They've set up traps of their own making, ways to test your strength. When you go in, there's a single passageway straight across to a series of stone pillars. If one of them calls to you, walk towards it, stand in front of it and touch the pillar when you're ready. The test will be revealed to you. If you pass, you will be let out of the stone and return to us with a mark on your hand from the stone. In our history, one only has survived fourteen days, and it is more common to survive four. If you come out of your pillar stone riding a dragon, it is yours. You will know."

Whispers echo and Catherine flashes me an excited but nervous smile.

"It's important you do not go off the path. It's there for a reason. If none of the pillars call to you, walk out as quickly as you possibly can, back to the door. Run if you want to live. The Decidere door only opens on Sundays, so you will have a week between each Decidere to rest and train." Daegan looks up at the dragon statue. "The ancient fae kings of our dynasties set up the Decidere many years ago with the dragons so our people would forever be blessed with riders. They built our great cities with endless caverns filled with dragon pillars. Any time a fae turned twenty-one, they were taken down there to be tested, and our riders filled the skies. Of course, these times have gone and our cities with them, apparently." Gasps echo and so many eyes fall on me. "But this does not mean that we will not find a way forward through the darkness and escape this prison. The more riders we have, the better chance we have when we finally are freed from this to take back our world. Freedom is close, my friends and family. Our dynasty will rule in fire and blood, and the vampyres will be destroyed!"

Cheers and shouts mix with the beat of the drums until it is echoing. The cheering doesn't stop as Daegan steps aside and we make a line to the door. I follow closely behind Catherine, and Ziven's man stays right at my back. I look over once more at Ziven, and he flashes me a cruel smirk before I face away. He hates me and I'm not a fan of him either, the psychopath. What is wrong with him? It's like he singled me out as his enemy before we even spoke.

My legs feel like they are full of lead as I walk through the open stone door and into a damp-smelling tunnel. My heart begins to race so fast that I hear it in my ears, hear it rattling my soul. What am I doing? I should run away. I should absolutely run away. I know I won't get very far, but I'm literally walking to my death by dragon.

The curious side of me wants to see a dragon, not just a statue or a drawing in a book. I'm not sure it's worth dying for, though. The tunnel leads to a dug-out hollow in the stone. There are big gaps on either side of a bridge to the other side, easily wide enough for five people to walk across. On the other side are pillars, rows and rows of tall rectangular pillars that must be over ten feet tall. There's nothing on them, they're just smooth stone that is slightly pushed into the ground. My eyes flicker round the edges of the cave before a roar echoes, so close and loud that cracks form in the walls and bits of rock tumble from the ceiling, crashing at my feet.

Jumping back, I see the stone door is shut behind us, and the roar echoes again, getting louder and causing more rocks to fall. People scream and scatter, and someone slams into my shoulder, shoving me to the ground. I lift my head to see rocks crushing people as they run for the pillars. I have to get to the pillars, *get up, Story*. I push off the ground, running straight to the bridge just as a dragon lands right on top of the side of the bridge, roaring loudly and shaking everything. It's huge, absolutely massive, and made of pure crackled stone. I don't know what I was expecting, but not this. Massive stone wings spread out on either side of the dragon. All over its back is crusted-over stone, and a long lumpy tail has sharp rocks on its end. It roars as its black eyes finally drop and narrow. Red embers flicker off its forked tongue as it opens its mouth, and I feel frozen to my spot.

A stream of burning hot fire sprays out of its mouth, right into the bridge, and it instantly burns up three people before they can even scream. The horrid smell of burning flesh fills my nose as I suck in a breath, taking several steps back only to bump into someone. I turn around to find the man from the Moon Dynasty, Ziven's friend. He is calm, collected, as he grabs my upper arms in a tight grip, and I struggle to move at all. He leans into me, his deep voice nothing but cruel. "King Ziven expressed how he hoped you die from this."

"Wait—" He picks me up and throws me straight off the edge of the bridge, into the endless cold air.

Made in the USA
Coppell, TX
20 November 2024

40587550R00218